開企，

是一個開頭，它可以是一句美好的引言、
未完待續的逗點、享受美好後滿足的句點，
新鮮的體驗、大膽的冒險、嶄新的方向，
是一趟有你共同參與的奇妙旅程。

超夯！英文流行語
Recent Buzzwords
這樣說最潮
WOW

User's Guide

使用說明

說英文也要趕流行，
跳脫制式英語，這樣說才跟得上時代！

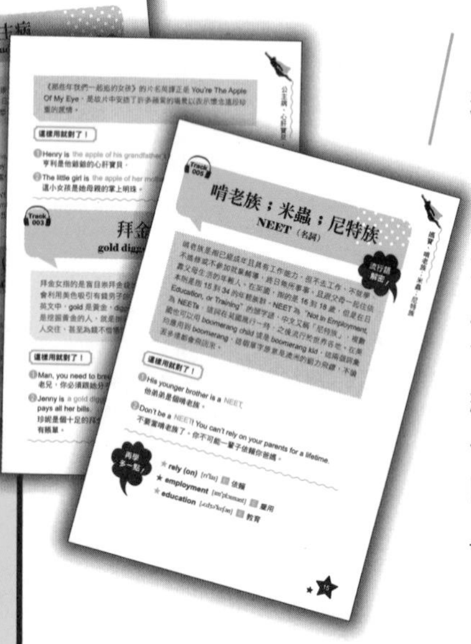

公主病
princess syndrome

心肝寶貝
the apple of my eye

拜金女
gold digger

啃老族；米蟲；尼特族
NEET（名詞）

18 種聊天情境，近 400 個超夯流行語，現學現用！

跟朋友聊天打屁，誰還要用老掉牙的八股文？！想要輕鬆打入老外社交圈，讓老外驚呼你超屌，那就快來學這些流行語！電腦要update、手機平板要update、聊天話題當然也要隨時update，本書教你：網紅、放閃、公主病、媽寶、魯蛇、富二代、小三、啃老族……讓你隨時都能跟外國朋友聊最新、最八卦的話題，真正跟得上流行趨勢！

超夯流行語大解密，讓你一看就懂！

用簡單扼要的方式針對每一則流行語進行最獨一無二的解說，內容涵蓋流行語的使用時機、英文單字的用法、使用注意事項、流行語由來、相關流行語……等等，最淺顯易懂的剖析，讓你對流行語有更深入的了解！

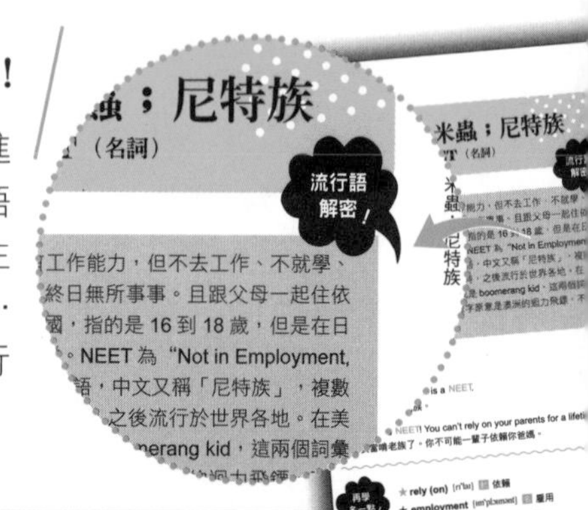

看例句
學超夯流行語，這樣用就對了！

好不容易學了流行語，當然要知道怎麼使用，每一則流行語皆以2-3個生活常用句輔助學習，讓你親身感受這些流行語要如何實際應用在我們的日常生活當中，下次跟老外聊天就立馬用上這些超夯流行語，不用瞎掰硬扯，擺脫舌頭打結，還能看到老外嚇到說不出話，驚嘆你居然連這句都會說！

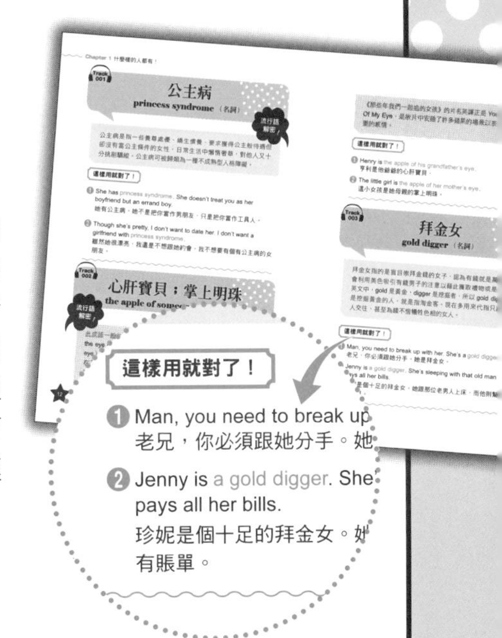

流行語學了不會說？
放心，外師親錄 MP3 說給你聽

外師親錄純正美語發音，書內所有流行語及例句通通說給你聽，本書特別採用「老外日常說話速度」錄音，希望幫助使用者預先熟悉外國人平日交談時的語速及音調的抑揚頓挫，隨時隨地累積英聽實力，真正聽到老外說英語時，自然而然能聽懂，保證不慌亂。

你知道語言也講究流行感嗎？想當一個走在時尚潮流的人，不僅穿著打扮講流行，個人的說話方式及談吐，也會影響別人對你的觀感，過時的語言不僅無法有效溝通，還可能讓對方臉上三條線，試想跟朋友聊天時，你如果突然冒出一句文言文，對方應該哭笑不得，覺得你很假掰，或認為你是從火星來的。

本書收錄的流行語都是時下日常生活中、社群媒體上、甚至新聞報導中經常使用的用語，冠以「最夯」二字自是恰到好處、名實相符。這些流行語的英文，有一部份是英文中已經存在、道道地地的慣用語，並非中文的翻譯或意譯。所以，當你跟老美說 "friend zone" 時，他們都知道你是要表達「好人卡」的意思；同樣地，當你說 "bingo wings" 時，他們也知道你指的是「蝴蝶袖」。書中的流行語也有一部分是近幾年才突然被廣泛使用，譬如："NEET" 是表示近年被廣泛討論的社會議題「啃老族」；又或者 "Internet celebrity"，則是最近新聞或臉書上很常被提及的「網紅」之意。

本書所收錄的近 400 個最夯流行語，包括「靠爸族」(daddy's boy/girl)、「放閃」(PDA)、「小鮮肉」(hunk)、

「夜店咖」(club rat)、「公主病」(princess syndrome)、「窮忙族、薪貧族」(the working poor)、「渣男」(fuckboy)、「魯蛇」(loser) 、「高人氣」(high popularity)等等，其中若干流行語有兩種或兩種以上的英文講法，更予以詳細的解釋並輔以例句來區分它們之間的不同，讓讀者能瞭解其細微之差異及確實的意含。例如：「車震」有 amomaxia 和 dogging 兩種說法，但兩者含意有別，我們亦會在書中做詳細介紹。此外，每個流行語都有必要的說明，俾讓讀者可以學到相關用語或知識，而每個流行語還提供至少兩個例句，讓讀者能進一步瞭解它們的實際用法。

流行語推陳出新，每隔一段時間就會有新的流行語出現。但並非所有流行語都有相對應的英文用語，這些流行語就成了本書的「漏網之魚」，讓人頗感遺憾，希望日後能予以補齊。任何書籍都無法十全十美，本書亦然，若有疏漏之處，歡迎批評指教。

☞ 作者英文學習網站：

1. 網路翻譯家：https://cybertranslator.idv.tw

2. 英文資訊交流網：https://blog.cybertranslator.idv.tw

2017年12月

Contents

目錄

Chapter

1

什麼樣的人都有！

公主病

princess syndrome（名詞）

流行語解密！

公主病是指一些養尊處優、嬌生慣養、要求獲得公主般待遇但卻沒有當公主條件的女性，日常生活中懶惰奢華，對他人又十分挑剔驕縱。公主病可被歸類為一種不成熟型人格障礙。

這樣用就對了！

1. She has princess syndrome. She doesn't treat you as her boyfriend but an errand boy.
   她有公主病。她不是把你當作男朋友，只是把你當作工具人。

2. Though she's pretty, I don't want to date her. I don't want a girlfriend with princess syndrome.
   雖然她很漂亮，我還是不想跟她約會。我不想要有個有公主病的女朋友。

Track 002

心肝寶貝；掌上明珠

the apple of someone's eye（名詞）

流行語解密！

此成語一般位在 be 動詞之後，屬慣用法，不可寫成 the apple of the eye of someone，其中的 apple 原指「瞳孔」（pupil of the eye），表示某人對自己非常重要，猶如自己的眼珠一樣珍貴。在英文中除了表示「掌上明珠」這種對女兒的珍愛，也可以用來表達對情人或其他重要的人的呵護。而當年紅遍全台的電影

《那些年我們一起追的女孩》的片名英譯正是 You're The Apple Of My Eye，是故片中安插了許多蘋果的場景以表示懷念這段珍重的感情。

這樣用就對了！

1. Henry is the apple of his grandfather's eye.
亨利是他爺爺的心肝寶貝。

2. The little girl is the apple of her mother's eye.
這小女孩是她母親的掌上明珠。

Track 003

拜金女

gold digger（名詞）

流行語解密！

拜金女指的是盲目崇拜金錢的女子，認為有錢就是萬能，並且會利用美色吸引有錢男子的注意以藉此獲取禮物或是錢財。在英文中，gold 是黃金，digger 是挖掘者，所以 gold digger 本意是挖掘黃金的人，就是指淘金客。現在多用來代指只跟有錢男人交往、甚至為錢不惜犧牲色相的女人。

這樣用就對了！

1. Man, you need to break up with her. She's a gold digger.
老兄，你必須跟她分手。她是拜金女。

2. Jenny is a gold digger. She's sleeping with that old man and he pays all her bills.
珍妮是個十足的拜金女。她跟那位老男人上床，而他則幫她支付所有賬單。

媽寶

mama's boy, momma's boy, mummy's boy（名詞）

流行語解密！

媽寶指的是已經成年了，但是什麼都要問媽媽的意見，無主見、無責任感，生活大小事情都要媽媽打理，且缺乏生活自理能力的人，通常指的是男性。mama's boy 和 momma's boy 為美式拼法，而 mummy's boy 為英式拼法。除了媽寶的意思外，它們還意為「沒有男子氣概的男人」，使用時須從上下文判斷意思。

這樣用就對了！

1. He was my Mr. Right until I realized he was a mama's boy.
   在我知道他是個媽寶之前我都以為他是我的白馬王子。

2. I received a phone call from Dean's parents last night. I won't tell him more about work, because he is a momma's boy.
   昨晚我接到迪恩父母打來的電話。我不會再跟他討論工作，因為他是個媽寶。

3. You're such a mummy's boy.
   你真是個媽寶。

★ **Mr. Right** [ˋmɪstɚ][raɪt] 名 白馬王子

★ **realize** [ˋriə͵laɪz] 動 實現、瞭解

啃老族；米蟲；尼特族

NEET（名詞）

流行語解密！

啃老族是指已經成年且具有工作能力，但不去工作、不就學、不進修或不參加就業輔導，終日無所事事。且跟父母一起住依靠父母生活的年輕人。在英國，指的是 16 到 18 歲，但是在日本則是指 15 到 34 的年輕族群。NEET 為 "Not in Employment, Education, or Training" 的頭字語，中文又稱「尼特族」，複數為 NEETs，這詞在英國風行一時，之後流行於世界各地。在美國也可以用 boomerang child 或是 boomerang kid，這兩個詞彙均應用到 boomerang，這個單字原意是澳洲的迴力飛鏢，不論丟多遠都會飛回來。

這樣用就對了！

1. His younger brother is a NEET.
   他弟弟是個啃老族。

2. Don't be a NEET! You can't rely on your parents for a lifetime.
   不要當啃老族了。你不可能一輩子依賴你爸媽。

★ **rely (on)** [rɪˋlaɪ] 動 依賴

★ **employment** [ɪmˋplɔɪmənt] 名 雇用

★ **education** [ˌɛdʒəˋkeʃən] 名 教育

靠爸族

daddy's boy/girl （名詞）

流行語解密！

靠爸族指的是利用父親或是家中其他長輩的關係，而在工作上比他人有更多機會，在大陸又稱「拼爹」。這詞在台灣會暴紅，是因為歌手劉子千靠著父親資深音樂人劉家昌的特殊關係，才進入音樂界，而引起熱烈討論。之後這詞廣泛應用在嘲弄政商以及演藝等界，靠著父親的關係而得到成就的人。在英文中，daddy's boy 也可以指稱受到父親影響而特異表現出男子氣概的男孩，而 daddy's girl 則有「被爸爸寵壞」的意味。

這樣用就對了！

1. That daddy's boy just got a new mansion.
   那個靠爸族剛得到一棟豪宅。
2. I don't want to travel abroad with you because I'm not a daddy's girl.
   我不要跟你一起出國，我不是靠爸族。

富二代

rich second generation （名詞）

流行語解密！

眾所周知，「富二代」指的就是出生自富裕家庭的第二代，即有錢父母的小孩 (the children of wealthy parents)，因為富二代特別指稱在中國地區，所以可以用中文直接音譯 Fuerdai。較精準的英文則是 rich second generation，這詞並無貶義，而 second generation 除了指「第二代」，也可以用來代指新一代的電子產品。

這樣用就對了！

1. According to a survey, nearly 60 percent of college girls in China want to marry the "rich second generation."
根據一項調查，在中國有近 60 % 的女大生想嫁給富二代。

2. The rich second generation is always flaunting their wealth.
富二代老是炫富。

3. He is the rich second generation, but he works hard to succeed.
他是富二代，但是他很努力才獲得成功。

Track 008

高富帥

tall, rich, and handsome（形容詞）

流行語解密！

多指那些身材高大、富有、帥氣的男生，他們擁有名車，豪宅，而且收入普遍都很高。高富帥的相反詞是魯蛇，指的是矮窮醜的男性。在英文中，除了 tall, rich and handsome 之外，privileged 也有此意味，指的是有特殊優勢的人。或是直接用中文音譯成 Gaofushuai，專指在中國地區高富帥的男性。

這樣用就對了！

1. I want to marry someone tall, rich, and handsome.
我想要嫁給高富帥。

2. Jodi doesn't want to marry a tall, rich, and handsome man.
喬蒂不想要嫁個高富帥的男人。

型男；花美男

metrosexual （名詞）

流行語解密！

花美男指男生像是花一樣漂亮，擁有白皙的肌膚、俊秀的面龐，近年來在東亞流行起來。在英文中會用 metrosexual 來代指花美男，這個字是由“metro-”（都市）和 sexual（性別）組合而成。它首次出現在 1994 年，為英國作家兼社會評論家馬克 ・ 辛普森 (Mark Simpson) 所創造，指的是重視外貌且具有美感的都會男子。它的相關字 metrosexuality（名詞）則意為「花美男注重儀表、穿著時尚、品嚐美食、愛好生活享樂的態度和風格」。

這樣用就對了！

1. Michael is considered a metrosexual.
   麥可被認為是個花美男。

2. A metrosexual can usually attract a lot of women.
   型男往往能吸引許多女性。

Track 010

師奶殺手；帥哥

lady killer （名詞）

流行語解密！

「師奶」在粵語中是已婚婦女的意思，以往特別指稱家庭主婦且帶有貶義，但現在這詞比較中性，單純的指中年婦女。師奶殺手則是指長得非常帥，對年長女性特別有吸引力的男性。要特別注意的是，lady killer 除了可以指因為行為舉止得當而對女性特別有吸引力的男性，還隱含有「與許多女性有性關係」的意味。

這樣用就對了！

1. David Beckham is extremely charming for my mother. I think he is more like a lady killer.
我媽覺得貝克漢很帥又很迷人。我覺得他比較像是個師奶殺手。

2. He's something of a lady killer.
他算得上是個帥哥。

Track 011

陽光型男孩

boy with a sunny disposition/ personality （名詞）

流行語解密！

陽光男孩指的是性格開朗，且喜歡運動、喜歡戶外活動的男孩，且個性有擔當、有領導能力還具有紳士風度，給人溫暖且可靠的感覺。在英文中會用 a sunny disposition/personality 表達「陽光型性格」，亦即「開朗的性格」。當然了，我們亦可將 boy 改為 girl 來表達「陽光型女孩」的意思。另外在國外也很常用 sportive，是擅長運動的意思，也隱含有「陽光型」的意味。

這樣用就對了！

1. Pan is a smart boy with a sunny disposition. Many girls are into him.
潘是個聰明的陽光型男孩，很多女生都很喜歡他。

2. Jennifer is such a cute girl with a sunny personality.
珍妮佛真的是個可愛又陽光的女孩。

宅男／女；肥宅

homebody（名詞）; fat nerd（名詞）

流行語解密！

宅男是來自日本的流行語，指喜歡待在家裡，而不喜歡出門與人相處，特別指沉迷於線上遊戲的男性，不過近年來也有「宅女」這稱呼用來形容足不出戶的女性。在英文中有 homebody 這詞指喜歡待在家的人，但這詞較為正面，有顧家、戀家的意味。此外，亦可用 shut-in 來表示，shut in 當動詞時，有「關緊閉」的意思。而 shut-in 還可以當形容詞使用。只是 shut-in 沒有 homebody 那麼常用。比宅男更負面的稱呼是「肥宅」，表示足不出戶到身材都變形了，這個字的英文通常會用 fat nerd，nerd 是「怪人」的意思，fat nerd 就是又肥又怪的「肥宅」了。

這樣用就對了！

1. I'm a homebody. I don't want to do anything but stay at home and play computer games.
我是宅男，除了待在家打電動我什麼都不想做。

2. Don't ask her to go shopping with us, because she's a homebody who doesn't like to go out.
別叫她來跟我們一起逛街，因為她是個不愛出門的宅女。

★ **nerd** [ˋnɝd] 名 （俚語）笨蛋，討人厭的傢伙

魯蛇／滷蛇

loser（名詞）

流行語解密！

在台灣，魯蛇來自英文 loser，失敗者的意思，魯蛇通常指收入不高、長相平凡、且沒有女朋友的男性。在 2013 年蛇年的時候「魯蛇」一詞大紅，此詞衍生出許多相關的詞彙，例如「魯妹」專指女魯蛇，或是「滷味很重」指的是已經當魯蛇很久，特別是指一直都沒有女朋友的魯蛇。魯蛇的相反詞是溫拿 (winner)，指的是有權勢、及外貌傑出的交往對象者，但相較魯蛇，溫拿的使用範圍較小。

這樣用就對了！

1. He has never had a girlfriend, but he works hard to not be a loser.
   他從來沒有交過女朋友，但他很努力不要變成魯蛇。

2. You were dumped? Welcome back to the group of losers.
   你被甩了？歡迎回到魯蛇的行列。

★ **dump** [dʌmp] 動 拋下／名 垃圾場

▶延伸片語：**dump the garbage** 倒垃圾

A 咖；B 咖；C 咖

A-list; B-list; C-list（名詞）（形容詞）

流行語解密！

數年前，美國一位名叫 James Ulmer 的娛樂記者自創一項量尺來評量電影明星的身價。他把這個量尺叫做 Ulmer Scale，而 Ulmer 量尺出人意表地竟變得非常受歡迎、廣為流行，現在有許多人使用這一量尺。根據 Ulmer 量尺，最紅的影星、演員如湯姆漢克 (Tom Hanks) 是 A-list，也就是 A 咖，至於比這些身價最高的影星、演員略差一截者就叫做 B-list，即 B 咖，而行情再往下探的三流影星、演員則是 C-list，即 C 咖。現在除了在演藝界，日常生活中也會使用 A 咖、B 咖、C 咖來形容人的表現是一流、二流或是三流。

這樣用就對了！

1. Meryl Streep is an A-list.
   梅莉史翠普是 A 咖。

2. He is a B-list actor.
   他是個 B 咖演員。

一家之主

wear the pants/trousers（動詞）

流行語解密！

「一家之主」這一詞出自明朝馮夢龍的《醒世恆言》，指的是一個家庭中作主的人，也隱含有負責的意思。在傳統父權社會下往往是一個家的男主人，現在使用上較無性別限制。這詞後面往往接 in one's family/house。

這樣用就對了！

1. Sandy seems to wear the pants in her family and is always telling her husband what to do.
珊蒂似乎是她家的一家之主，她老是對她先生頤指氣使。

2. There's no doubt about who wears the pants in their house since he has all the rights.
既然他都有全部的權力，他們家裡誰是一家之主已無庸置疑。

★ **trousers** [ˋtrauzɚz] 名 褲子

★ **doubt** [daut] 名 疑問／動 懷疑

▶延伸片語：**beyond doubt** 無疑地、不容懷疑

★ **have/has all the rights** 片 有全部的權力

女漢子

tomboy（名詞）, cowgirl（名詞）

流行語解密！

女漢子是具有陽剛氣質的女性，行為舉止豪放且穿著中性。有人將 tomboy 翻譯為「男人婆」，但是不同於男人婆，tomboy 並無歧視意味。在台灣，曾經有立委用這詞質詢部長，並且聲稱 tomboy 是女同性戀的意思，因而廣被討論。其實台灣早期的女同性戀把這字拿來代指女同性戀中比較偏向陽剛氣質的一方，也是日後所衍生的 T（或稱「踢」，或是直譯「湯包」），相對於較陰性氣質的 P (pure) 或稱作「婆」。此外，英文還有一個字 cowgirl 是牛仔女孩，也有女漢子的意味，tomboy 僅當名詞用，它的形容詞是 tomboyish。

這樣用就對了！

1. Jean has always been tomboyish. She likes wearing boy's clothes.
   吉恩一直很男子氣，她喜歡穿男裝。
2. She's a cowgirl! She can do everything by herself.
   她真是個女漢子！她什麼都可以自己來。

Track
017

小鮮肉；猛男

hunk（名詞）

流行語解密！

hunk 這詞彙本身指的是「一大塊」，可以用在 a hunk of evidence（一個強大的證據）。在俚語中，hunk 亦指性感的男模，尤指身材姣好、英俊挺拔，拍攝內衣廣告的男模。中文中的「小鮮肉」則是指年輕且壯美的男性。如果有人非要強調「小」（年輕的意思）這個字的話，那麼可以用 hunky boy 來表示「小鮮肉」，殆無爭議。

這樣用就對了！

1. Girls crowded into the plaza because there were many hunks chiseled with six-pack abs.
   女孩們蜂擁進廣場，因為這邊有很多小鮮肉，他們都有如鑿刻般的六塊肌。
2. Mr. Green is a hunk. I think he must work as a model.
   格林先生是一位猛男！我想他一定是男模。

Track 018

小狼狗

toy boy（名詞）

流行語解密！

小狼狗跟「老王」、「小白臉」、「情夫」意思雷同，指的是女性外遇的對象，這詞往往有靠女方養的意味。另外，因為傳說中狼狗性能力強，所以小狼狗這一詞也可以指性能力強而被年長女性包養的年輕男性。這詞在英文中比較強調一段感情中女方靠經濟能力讓男性成為性玩物，所以不一定是指外遇的關係。也可以寫成 boy toy。除了用在非婚關係中，姊弟戀修成正果後，這位「大姊」的「小老公」，英文叫做 toy boy husband。

這樣用就對了！

1. He's her new toy boy.
   他是她新交的小狼狗。
2. Do you know Kate's new toy boy?
   你認識凱特新交的小狼狗嗎？

小白臉

gigolo（名詞）

流行語解密！

小白臉是指外貌姣好，長相斯文清秀的男子，通常肌膚白皙，因而被稱作「小白臉」，這些男子會利用姣好的外貌來吸引年長女性包養。現在也會用這詞代指靠女人而活的男人。在英文可以用 gigolo，這個字亦意為「舞男；男妓」，但是這詞較為不雅，使用時必須謹慎。複數為 gigolos。

這樣用就對了！

1. The woman had a gigolo but her husband knows nothing about it.
   那個女人養了小白臉但是她丈夫完全不知情。

2. Jimmy just got himself a new sugar mommy. Damn that guy's such a gigolo!
   吉米剛找到一位新的乾媽。該死，那傢伙真是個小白臉。

★ **sugar mommy/daddy** 片 乾媽／乾爹

★ **damn** [dæm] 動 指責、輕蔑

渣男

fuckboy, fuck boy（名詞）

流行語解密！

渣男也是近年來從網路興起的詞彙，意思是始亂終棄、玩弄別人感情、對感情不專一的男性。渣這詞也可以當作形容詞，形容男性對感情不負責的態度。在英文也有類似的網路用語：fuckboy。fuck boy 或是避免髒話而寫成 f-boy，意思也是追求性愛，對感情不專一且不尊重女性的男性，然而這詞也有可能指的是總是做蠢事的男性。

這樣用就對了！

1. Your girlfriend is the best girl in the world. Be faithful to her. Don't be a fuck boy again.

   你女朋友是世界上最好的女孩了。對她認真點，不要再當個渣男。

2. He asks you to pay the bill for him. He cheats on you many times. He has never been nice to you. Don't you know he is a fuckboy? Don't be sad because he leaves you.

   他總是要你幫他買單，他出軌那麼多次，他從來沒有對你好過，這樣你還不知道他是個渣男嗎？不要因為他離開你而難過。

★ **faithful** [ˋfeθfəl] 形 忠實的、耿直的、可靠的

小三

mistress（名詞）

流行語解密！

小三是丈夫外遇的對象，因為是第三者所以稱做「小三」。因為台灣的電視劇《犀利人妻》講述著丈夫外遇妻子的表妹，使得「小三」這詞暴紅。「小三」通常是看起來清純可愛惹人疼惜，但橫刀奪愛破壞別人家庭時毫不手軟，電視中的台詞「在愛情中，不被愛的人才是第三者」也成為小三的經典名言。

這樣用就對了！

1. He has a mistress in Hong Kong.
   他在香港有小三。

2. Though Professor Smith is a hen-pecked husband, he has a mistress.
   史密斯教授雖然很怕老婆，但他卻敢背地裡有小三。

老少配

May-December romance（名詞）

流行語解密！

May 是五月，是百花盛開青春正旺的時候，而 December 是十二月，則是百木蕭條暮遲之年，所以 May-December romance 就是老少配。May-December romance 不一定是男大女小或是女大男小，亦可用 May-December relationship 或是 May-December love 來表示。

這樣用就對了！

1. Being able to compromise is key to succeeding in having a May-December romance.
   能夠妥協是老少配成功的關鍵。

2. The biggest challenge that people who are in a May-December relationship face is how to gain acceptance from family members and friends.
   老少配所面臨的最大挑戰，就是如何獲得家人和朋友的接受。

姊弟戀

tadpoling（名詞）

流行語解密！

tadpoling 的動詞為 tadpole，意為「姊弟戀」。tadpole 亦可當名詞用，意為「蝌蚪」。事實上，tadpoling 真正的含義是，熟女與相差至少十歲的年下男交往。姊弟戀中的熟女就叫做 tadpoler。英文中還有一個字可以稱呼這種想要跟年紀比自己小很多的男子發生關係的中年婦女，那就是 cougar（原義為「美洲獅」）。

這樣用就對了！

1. Tadpoling is not accepted by most people.
   姊弟戀不為大多數人所接受。

2. Anna is tadpoling by dating such a young man.
   安娜跟這麼年輕的男生約會，是姊弟戀。

★ **accept** [ək`sɛpt] 動 接受

◀相關字：**acceptable** [ək`sɛptəbl̩] 形 可接受的／**acceptance** [ək`sɛptəns] 名 接受

吃軟飯

sponge off women （動詞）

流行語解密！

sponge 是海綿的意思，所以 sponge off 意思是「用海綿擦拭」。在口語上 sponge off (somebody) 意為「依賴（某人）生活」，帶有「白吃白喝」的意味。當你依靠女人生活 sponge off women 時，那就是「吃軟飯」。

這樣用就對了！

1. Let's go to Tokyo, we can always sponge off my sister there.
   我們去東京吧，我們在那裡可以一直依靠我妹妹生活。

2. Bill sponges off women and never has to work.
   比爾吃軟飯，從來不用工作。

3. She is filing for divorce because her husband not only sponges off her but also beats her.
   她正要離婚因為她丈夫不只吃軟飯還會打她。

★ **file** [faɪl] 動 申請 名 檔案

★ **divorce** [də`vors] 名 離婚、解除婚約／動 使離婚、離婚

▶延伸片語：**divorce oneself from...** 與……離婚

Chapter 2

我的感情
我做主！

單戀；單相思

unrequited love （名詞）

流行語解密！

單戀；單相思亦可用 one-sided love 來表示。unrequited 這個形容詞意為「單相思的」，而 unrequited love 也可以用來表達「暗戀」的意思。

這樣用就對了！

1. John has unrequited love for a girl in his class.
約翰單戀他班上一個女孩。

2. Henry has been tortured by his unrequited love for that married colleague.
亨利一直為他單戀那位已婚同事所苦。

3. I love him, but he loves her. One-sided love surely sucks.
我愛他，但他卻愛她。單戀真是糟透了。

★ **unrequited** [ʌnˋrikwɪətɪd] 形 得不到回報的

★ **torture** [ˋtɔrtʃɚ] 動 痛苦

★ **colleague** [ˋkɑlig] 名 同事

想抓住男人的心，先抓住男人的胃

The way to a man's heart is through his stomach.

流行語解密！

這是道道地地的英文俗諺，直譯是「男人的胃通往他的心」，跟中文「想抓住男人的心，先抓住男人的胃」意思一樣。

這樣用就對了！

1. My mother told me the way to a man's heart is through his stomach, so I learned how to cook.
   我媽告訴我想抓住男人的心，先抓住男人的胃，所以我就學煮飯。

2. She made an effort, but it is not always true that the way to a man's heart is through his stomach.
   她很努力，但是抓住男人的胃不一定能抓住他的心。

再學多一點！

★ **make an effort** 片 用盡全力

★ **stomach**  名 1. 腹肌
2. 胃

對某人有好感

have a crush on someone（動詞）

流行語解密！

若動詞是用 harbor（停靠），變成 harbor a crush on 也是迷戀的意思，很常會加上 secret 變成 harbor a secret crush on someone 意思則是「偷偷迷戀某人」。若動詞是用 develop 來代替，變成 develop a crush on someone 則是「對某人產生好感」。crush 是迷戀的意思，可能只是一時的意亂情迷，也可以是真心的喜歡，通常都是在剛認識不久時的好感。此外，crush 也可以指著迷的對象。

這樣用就對了！

1. She used to have a massive crush on her English teacher in high school.
   她高中時曾經瘋狂地迷戀她的英文老師。

2. Daniel has developed a crush on Nicole.
   丹尼爾已對妮可產生好感。

Track
028

故作矜持

play hard to get（動詞）

流行語解密！

這成語通常指男女交往中對異性的故作矜持或是在工作等方面的欲擒故縱。

這樣用就對了！

1. Why don't you return any of his messages? Are you playing hard to get?
為何妳都不回他的訊息呢？妳是故作矜持嗎？

2. Cathy would not accept the job. She plays hard to get in the hope of being offered more money.
凱西不會接受這工作，她會欲擒故縱以期獲得較高的薪資。

Track 029

來電

chemistry （名詞）

流行語解密！

chemistry 是化學的意思，有化學變化就是來電了。表達兩人來電，除 chemistry 外，我們亦可用 sparks（火花）來表達相同的意思，例如：The first time I kissed my girlfriend I saw sparks flying around.（我第一次吻我女友時，我感到火花四濺。）要注意的是，have chemistry 除了指在感情上的來電，也可以說兩人講話投機、合拍、有默契等。

這樣用就對了！

1. There's no chemistry between Mary and Bill.
瑪麗和比爾不來電。

2. The chemistry between Amy and John was obvious.
艾美和約翰顯然很來電。

放電；拋媚眼

make eyes at someone（動詞）

流行語解密！

這句英文的完整意思是「對某人放電；對某人拋媚眼」。這邊的 eye 是「電眼」的意思，也可以用 give someone the eye，例如：She has given him the eye since he spoke.（從他開口說話，她就一直對他放電。）要注意 give someone the eye 除了放電，還有「使眼色」的意思喔，例如：My mom gave me the eye to stop me from telling him the truth.（我媽對我使眼色，要我不要跟他說實情。）

這樣用就對了！

1. Gary tried to make eyes at the pretty girl.
蓋瑞試圖對那漂亮的女孩亂放電。

2. Don't make eyes at my daughter!
不准對我女兒放電！

放閃

PDA (public display of affection)

（名詞）

流行語解密！

在中文中說的放閃，意思是情侶在眾人面前有親密舉動秀恩愛，讓周邊的人不自在，後來也衍生出一些相關的用法，像是：閃瞎我的眼睛，另外在網路上還有其他用法，例如叫自己的男女朋友是閃光，或是閃光 get 表示交到男女朋友。在英文中有 PDA（public displays of affection）直譯是公開展現愛情，也就是中文的放閃囉！在英文中當名詞，可以當男女朋友或是曬恩愛。

這樣用就對了！

1. Is Joe her new PDA?
   喬伊是她新的閃光嗎？

2. My grandparents' PDA is even more intense than that of the youth!
   我祖父母比年輕人還閃！

★ **intense** [ɪnˋtɛns] 形 極度的、緊張的

▶延伸片語：**intense fall** 暴雨

▶相關詞：**intensify** [ɪnˋtɛnsə͵faɪ] 動 加強、增強／
intensity [ɪnˋtɛnsətɪ] 名 強度、強烈／
intensive [ɪnˋtɛnsɪv] 形 強烈的、密集的

Track 032

真命天子

Mr. Right （名詞）

流行語解密！

Mr. Right 就是心目中的理想男性伴侶，如意郎君，白馬王子，亦可用 Mr. Perfect 或 Prince Charming 來表示。相對的，若是心目中的理想女性伴侶，則可用 Mrs. Right, Miss Right 或是 Princess Charming。還有一個很常用的詞是 soul mate（靈魂伴侶），但是法律上的伴侶並不是用 mate 這個詞，而是 spouse（配偶）。

這樣用就對了！

1. Kevin was not the Mr. Right I was looking for.
   凱文不是我要找的真命天子。

2. Gary is my Prince Charming.
   蓋瑞是我的白馬王子。

Track 033

天生一對

a match made in heaven （名詞）

流行語解密！

天生一對就是天造地設的一對，亦即兩人非常速配，match 是「相配」、「婚姻」的意思，也可以說 a great match 或是將 match 當動詞，可以說 be perfectly matched。此外，若是用 marriage 組成 a marriage made in heaven 也是同樣的意思。類似的說法還有 be meant for each other（註定要在一起），

例如：We are meant for each other.（我們註定要在一起。）

這樣用就對了！

1. John and Mary are a match made in heaven.
約翰和瑪麗是天生一對。

2. They are a great match.
他們兩人非常適配。

Track 034

異地戀；遠距戀愛

long-distance relationship （名詞）

流行語解密！

異地戀，或是遠距離戀愛，指的是交往的兩人必須長期待在不同的地方。可以用 long-distance 或是沒有「-」的 long distance，意思是「長途的」，像是 long-distance call（長途電話）。除了 long-distance relationship 之外，也可以將 relationship 改成 love 變成 long-distance love。這裡的 relationship 意為「戀愛關係」，為可數名詞。

這樣用就對了！

1. I rejected him because I don't like long-distance relationship.
我拒絕他因為我不喜歡異地戀。

2. That's a long-distance relationship. It's so hard for me.
那是遠距戀愛，讓我很辛苦。

當電燈泡

play gooseberry（動詞）

流行語解密！

電燈泡的意思是當情侶約會時，硬要跟在旁邊的人。我們亦可用 to be a gooseberry 來表達相同的意思，但比較少用。gooseberry 本身的意思為「醋栗」。

這樣用就對了！

1. Jason and Anna are lovebirds, so I don't want to play gooseberry joining them in any social contexts.
   傑森和安娜是一對恩愛情侶，所以在任何社交場合我都不想當他們的電燈泡。

2. Amy and Bill asked me to go shopping with them, but I didn't want to play gooseberry.
   艾美和比爾邀我和他們一起去購物，但我不想當電燈泡。

3. I'm not going to the movies with you guys tonight, because I don't want to be a gooseberry.
   今晚我不跟你們去看電影，因為我不想當電燈泡。

老牛吃嫩草

rob the cradle （動詞）

流行語解密！

老牛吃嫩草中的「老牛」，意思是想要跟年紀比自己小很多的女子發生關係的中年男子，英文叫做 manther，是 man（男人）＋ panther（豹）所組成的字。在英文用 rob the cradle 表示老牛吃嫩草，其中 rob 是搶劫，cradle 是搖籃，搶奪搖籃的幼兒自然是老牛吃嫩草的意思了。

這樣用就對了！

1. Hugh Hefner is always robbing the cradle.
   海夫納常常老牛吃嫩草。 — 海夫納為《花花公子》（Playboy）雜誌的創辦人。

2. He's robbing the cradle! Jim's girlfriend is only 15.
   他是老牛吃嫩草！吉姆的女友只有 15 歲。

野獸美女配；牛糞鮮花配

over-chicked（形容詞）

流行語解密！

over-chicked 經常與 severely 和 seriously 這兩個副詞連用。除 over-chicked 外，英文還有一個用語可以表達完全相同的意思，那就是 A be way/well out of B's league，意為「B 配不上 A」，其中，way 當副詞用，意為「大大地；遠遠地」，與 well 同義。

這樣用就對了！

1. Have you seen Danny's girlfriend? He is seriously over-chicked!
你見過丹尼的女朋友了嗎，他是野獸配美女！

2. How did Harry ever get Paula to date him? He is really over-chicked.
哈利是怎樣讓寶拉跟他約會的？他真的是牛糞配鮮花。

3. Man, Caroline'll never go out with someone like you; she's way out of your league.
老兄，卡洛琳永遠不會跟你這樣的人交往；你配不上她。

好人卡

friend zone （名詞）

流行語解密！

好人卡起源於某男子向心儀的少女告白，但被對方以「你是個好人，但我們不能在一起」為由婉轉拒絕了。從此，「你是個好人」就成為男子被女子拒絕或女子被男子拒絕交往的代名詞。而「被發了好人卡」也就是被心儀的對象拒絕了的意思，至於付出很多但卻被對方拒絕交往的人，則被稱為「好人」。好人文化是 1990 年代之後在台灣等地發展出來的一種網路次文化，與男女交往問題有關。

這樣用就對了！

1. Brian was relegated to the friend zone by Emma last night.
   = Brian was placed in the friend zone by Emma last night.
   布萊恩昨晚被艾瑪發了好人卡。

2. Once you are in the friend zone, it is difficult to get out.
   你一旦獲得好人卡，就很難再當「壞人」了。

★ **zone** [zon] 名 區域

★ **relegate** [ˋrɛlə͵get] 動 歸類為……，貶謫

你不是我的菜

You're not my type. / You're not my cup of tea.

流行語解密！

cup of tea 源自於英國飲茶文化，最開始是用來形容「某一類的人」，現今多被用來指稱「喜歡的型」，可以指稱人或是東西，例如：Jazz music is my cup of tea.（爵士樂是我喜歡的類型。）You 可視情況改為適當的人稱主格或人名，如 He, She, Mary, John 等，而 my 同樣可視情況改為適當的人稱所有格，如 his, her 等。

這樣用就對了！

1. I like you, but you're not my type.
我喜歡你，但你不是我的菜。

2. He's such a hunk, but he's not my cup of tea.
他真是個猛男，但他不是我的菜。

Track 040

死會／活會

unavailable / available（形容詞）

流行語解密！

在男女交往或男女關係的上下文中，unavailable 是表示某人已有穩定交往的男友或女友、已訂婚或已婚，而反義詞 available 則表示某人並無穩定交往的男友或女友、未婚或目前單身。另外，我們亦會見到 emotionally unavailable 的用法，這是表示雖然你們還沒有交往或在一起，但你的心已經是屬於他或她了，即「心有所屬」。

這樣用就對了！

1. Cindy is available.
   辛蒂還沒死會。

2. Rachel is emotionally unavailable.
   瑞秋已心有所屬了。

精神出軌

emotionally cheat（動詞）

流行語解密！

精神出軌或精神外遇，是指某人實際上並沒有作出對不起對方的事，但心裡卻喜歡或想著別的男人或女人。此外，出軌叫做 have an affair with sb.，所以精神出軌也可以用 have an emotional affair with sb.，例如：I think my boyfriend has an emotional affair since he chats with Cindy happily all the time.（我覺得我男朋友精神出軌了，他總是很開心地跟辛蒂講話。）

這樣用就對了！

1. My boyfriend emotionally cheated on me.
   我男友精神出軌。

2. Paula's hubby usually emotionally cheats on her.
   寶拉的先生經常精神出軌。

劈腿

two-time（動詞）

流行語解密！

two-time someone = cheat on someone，意為「對伴侶不忠」。two-time 的過去式和過去分詞都是 two-timed，第三人稱單數動詞為 two-times，而現在分詞為 two-timing。劈腿的人叫做 two-timer。

這樣用就對了！

1. Are you sure Allen's not two-timing you?
   妳確定艾倫沒劈腿嗎？

2. Amy used to two-time her husband.
   艾美過去常背著她先生與人偷情。

3. Her boyfriend cheated on her.
   她男友劈腿了。

Track 043

頭頂綠綠的

cuckold（名詞）、（動詞）

流行語解密！

被戴綠帽的意思是妻子出軌，後來不僅限於妻子外遇，也可以用在男女朋友中被劈腿，戴綠帽在網路上還衍生出許多種說法，例如：頭頂綠綠的，綠光罩頂，都是被劈腿的意思。在英文中，cuckold 指稱被戴綠帽的人，也可以當動詞，意思是讓某人被戴綠帽，也很常用被動語態，表示「被戴綠帽」。

這樣用就對了！

1. My best friend cuckolded me.
我最好的朋友讓我戴綠帽了。

2. I am cuckold. My wife is having an affair with my supervisor. I don't know what to do.
我被戴綠帽了。我太太跟我上司有一腿，我不知道該怎麼辦。

3. Don't you know your wife is flirting with John? Hey, you are a cuckold!
你不知道你老婆跟約翰勾搭上了嗎？嘿，你頭頂綠綠的！

Track 044

天涯何處無芳草

There are plenty of fish in the sea.

流行語解密！

亦可寫成或說成 There are plenty of other fish in the sea. 或是 There are plenty more fish in the sea.

這樣用就對了！

1. When Jack broke up with Anna, I told him not to worry. There are plenty of fish in the sea.
當傑克和安娜分手時，我對他說別擔心。天涯何處無芳草。

2. Although there are plenty more fish in the sea, I haven't really got over her yet.
雖然天涯何處無芳草，但我真的還忘不了她。

Chapter 3

有沒有人氣
都要有
人際互動！

人氣
popularity （名詞）

流行語解密！

這個字就是 popular（受歡迎的；流行的）的名詞。人氣高是 high popularity，人氣低自然就是 low popularity 了。要增加人氣可以說 gain popularity，gain 是獲得的意思，也可以用在人氣上面。昔日高人氣，如今人氣不再，是謂過氣。過氣的人，尤其是過氣的名人，英文叫做 has-been。

這樣用就對了！

1. The singer's popularity is rising rapidly.
   這位歌手的人氣快速竄升。

2. The film star used to be famous and popular, but now she's just a has-been.
   這位電影明星過去名氣響亮、人氣紅不讓，但現已過氣。

Track 046

人脈
connection （名詞）

流行語解密！

connection 是連接、關係的意思，或是商務往來的「熟人」，所以也可以當「人脈」解釋。通常用複數 connections。「人脈廣」的英文可用 a lot of connections 或 well-connected （形容詞） 來表示。要講人脈，除了 connections，也可以用 contact（接觸、熟人）。

這樣用就對了！

1. I have a lot of connections. = I am well-connected.
我的人脈很廣。

2. Tracy used her party connections to get a government job.
崔西利用她的政黨人脈在政府部門謀得一份工作。

網紅

Internet celebrity （名詞）

流行語解密！

網紅是網路紅人的簡稱。Internet 是網際網路，celebrity 是名人的意思，合起來就是網路紅人了。在網路上暴紅的人，可能是因為拍攝 Youtube 影片的 youtuber，或是藉由部落格暴紅的人，也可以稱作 blogebrity，這個字是 blog ＋ celebrity 合成的。此外，還有一個詞 Internet meme，指的是網路上暴紅的東西，像是曾經紅遍一時的江南 style。而「暴紅」這詞的英文則是 go viral，viral 是病毒的意思，像病毒一樣擴散，就是暴紅囉！

這樣用就對了！

1. The Internet celebrity makes lots of money not merely because of her beauty but because of the power of her words.
那位網紅賺很多錢，不只是因為長得漂亮，還因為她文字很有力量。

2. To be a successful Internet celebrity, you need to learn how to make interesting videos and how to establish your own style.
要當一名成功的網紅，你不只要會拍攝有趣的影片，還要建立自己的風格。

大忙人

a busy bee （名詞）

流行語解密！

在較正式的英文，大忙人是 a busy man，在口語上也可以說 a busy bee。如果你是 a busy bee，那麼你一定 (as) busy as a bee 像蜜蜂一樣忙碌，非常忙碌。大忙人的相反詞是 jet-setter，指的是有錢有閒，時常搭乘噴射機周遊世界各地的富人。

這樣用就對了！

1. Felicia seems to be a very busy bee.
   費莉西亞看來是個大忙人。

2. All of us are not busy bees.
   我們都不是大忙人。

Track
049

只是普通朋友

just friends （名詞）

流行語解密！

「只是普通朋友」指的就是「不是男女朋友」。事實上，just friend 亦可當動詞用，意為「分手」（to break up with）。當男方或女方向對方說 “I just want to be a friend.” 時，意思就是「我只想跟你做普通朋友，不要（再）做男女朋友」。

這樣用就對了！

1. We’re just friends.
   我們只是普通朋友。

2 Wendy: I really like you a lot, Nick.

溫蒂：尼克，我真的很喜歡你。

Nick:I'm sorry. I like you too, but not like that. I hope we can still be just friends.

尼克：對不起，我也喜歡妳，但不是那種喜歡。我希望我們仍只是普通朋友。

3 I think Tom's girlfriend is going to just friend him.
我認為湯姆的女友要跟他分手。

Track 050

邊緣人

loner （名詞）

流行語解密！

邊緣人是沒有什麼朋友的人，在群體中也常常被忽略，在學校等團體生活中被視為特立獨行的怪人。在網路上流傳邊緣人的幾個特徵有：沒有人記得他的生日，所以只能自己幫自己慶生、課堂分組總是找不到組員等等。在英文中loner是lone（孤獨的）加上er（……的人）表示孤獨的人，本來loner是很中性的詞，可能是個性內向、獨立或是孤高自賞的人，只是現在這詞有越來越負面的趨向，跟中文的「邊緣人」雷同。

這樣用就對了！

1 I am not a loner. I just enjoy seeing a movie alone.
我不是邊緣人，我只是享受一個人看電影。

2 My son is called loner by his classmates. Do you think it is a kind of bullying?
我兒子被同學叫做邊緣人。你覺得這是霸凌嗎？

你人好好哦！你人真好！

How sweet of you! / You're a sweetheart!

流行語解密！

sweet 有「窩心」的意思，要用 sweet 讚美他人時，除了 You are sweet. 之外，也很常用 It's so sweet of you. 或是口語上用感歎句用法：How sweet of you! 不過 sweetheart 的這項用法已經有些過時。當然啦，主詞 you 可視不同情況改成適當的人稱或人名。

這樣用就對了！

1. You did me a big/great favor. How sweet of you!
   你幫了我一個大忙。你人好好哦！

2. Paul treated us all to dinner at an expensive restaurant. He's a real sweetheart!
   保羅請我們大家去一家昂貴餐館吃晚餐。他人真好！

Track 052

做壞人

play the heavy（動詞）

流行語解密！

heavy 在此當名詞用，意為「保鏢；打手；惡棍」。這個慣用語最初是指電影或戲劇中，男明星扮演反派角色。至於酒吧或夜店的保鏢，一般叫做 bouncer。

這樣用就對了！

❶ I'm a nice guy, but I play the heavy to my children.
我是個好人，但我對我小孩辦黑臉。

❷ My boss doesn't like to get rid of incompetent staff himself so he asks his secretary to play the heavy and fire them for him.
我的老闆不喜歡親自解僱不適任的員工，所以他要他的秘書去做壞人，替他開除那些人。

Track 053

我的錯；是我不好

my bad （名詞）

流行語解密！

「我的錯」的正式說法是：It's my fault.，但是在口語上會用 my bad，雖然文法不對，但俚語或口語仍使用廣泛。另外還有一個類似的用法是 You bad guy.（你這壞人。）也是文法錯誤的用法，但是口語上很常這樣用。

這樣用就對了！

❶ "You just spilled your wine on my new skirt!"
喂，你剛把紅酒潑在我新買的裙子上了！
"Oh. Sorry, that is my bad.
哦。對不起，那是我的錯。

❷ Yeah, that's all my bad.
是的，都是我不好。

吃閉門羹

slam the door in someone's face （動詞）

流行語解密！

吃閉門羹的意思是造訪他人時主人不在，或是遭到冷漠對待。在英文可以用 slam the door in someone's face，其中 slam 是「用力關上」的意思，這成語中的 slam 亦可用 shut 來代替，即 shut the door in someone's face，當著某人面把門甩上，意為「讓某人吃閉門羹」。

這樣用就對了！

1. We slammed the door in Jack's face since he was so rude when we interviewed him.
由於我們在面試傑克時他很沒禮貌，所以我們讓他吃了閉門羹。

2. The employees asked for only a small increase in pay, but the boss just shut the door in their face(s).
員工僅要求小幅加薪，但老闆卻讓他們吃了閉門羹。

Track 055

回請；回敬

return the compliment （動詞）

流行語解密！

有時亦寫成 return someone's compliment。compliment 是名詞或是動詞，意思是「讚美、恭維」，如果要說讚美他人可以說 He compliments on every woman in the party.（他讚美派對上每個女人。）後來 return the compliments 不只是字面上的「回敬他人的讚美」，也可以用在「回敬他人的好意」。

這樣用就對了！

1. He treats us so often that we really must return the compliment.
他常請我們吃飯，真的應該回請他才是。

2. Lori told me that my hair looked nice, so I returned her compliment and told her that her hair was lovely.
羅莉對我說，我的頭髮看起來很漂亮，所以我就回敬說，她的頭髮也很漂亮。

Track 056

若要人不知，除非己莫爲

murder will out

流行語解密！

out 在此當動詞用，意為「暴露；公開」。原本的意思是殺人犯行會曝光，因為傳統上有個迷信是殺人犯離死者的血最近，所以會招來厄運。後來這句話也可以用在其他地方，泛指做壞事一定會被發現。而 murderer 則是「殺人犯」的意思。

這樣用就對了！

1. Your wife will know about your affair with Phoebe sooner or later because murder will out.
你太太早晚會知道你跟菲比的婚外情，因為若要人不知，除非己莫為。

2. The President thought no one would ever discover his crime, but murder will out.
總統以為沒有人會發現他的罪行，但若要人不知，除非己莫為。

要就要，不要拉倒；要就要，不要就算了

take it or leave it（動詞）

流行語解密！

「要不要隨便你」或「接不接受隨便你」也是同義詞，同樣可用 take it or leave it 來表示。然而，這是主詞為第二人稱 you 或省略 you 的祈使句的情況。當主詞為第一或第三人稱時，take it or leave it（take 前面通常有語氣助動詞 can）的意思就變成了「要不要都可以；接不接受都可以」。

這樣用就對了！

1. I can lend you only 1,000 dollars. You can take it or leave it.
我只能借你一千元。要就要，不要拉倒。

2. A: I want pasta for dinner.
晚餐我要吃義大利麵。
B: There is only toast left. Take it or leave it.
現在只剩土司。不要就算了。

3. That's my final offer. Take it or leave it.
那是我的最後出價。要不要隨便你。

4. She likes cake, but she can take it or leave it.
她喜愛蛋糕，但她吃不吃都無所謂。

害群之馬

rotten apple （名詞）；black sheep （名詞）

流行語解密！

害群之馬就是團體中的敗類。rotten apple 字面意思為「爛蘋果」，亦可用 bad apple 來表達相同的意思。

這樣用就對了！

1. Most students in the class study hard but there are a few bad apples.
   班上大多數學生都很用功，但有少數害群之馬。

2. There are always some black sheep in the company.
   公司裡面總是有幾個害群之馬。

★ **rotten** [ˋrɑtn̩] 形 腐化的

▶延伸片語：**go rotten** 腐敗

★ **company** [ˋkʌmpənɪ] 名 公司、同伴

▶延伸片語：**A man is known by the company he keeps.** 近朱者赤，近墨者黑。

▶同義詞：**enterprise** [ˈɛntɚ͵praɪz] 名 公司

狼來了

cry wolf（動詞）

流行語解密！

源於伊索寓言（Aesop）：有個放羊的小孩經常喊「狼來了」來嚇唬鄰人，以此取樂。後來狼真的來了，但再也沒有人相信他的呼救聲，結果他的羊都被狼吃掉了。之後「喊狼來了」衍生出「說謊」的意思，而「放羊的孩子」（the boy who cried wolf）則是代表常說謊的人。

這樣用就對了！

1. The child is just crying wolf again. He didn't really get hurt.
   那小朋友只是又喊狼來了，他並沒有受傷。

2. Don't cry wolf too often. People will be annoyed and no one will believe you are in trouble.
   別常常喊狼來了，大家會覺得很煩，而且當你遇上麻煩時沒有人會相信你。

★ **annoyed** [əˋnɔɪ] 形 煩擾的

▶延伸片語：**be annoyed with sb. for sth.**
對（某人）為（某事）而生氣

▶相關詞：**annoy** 動 煩擾
annoying 形 令人煩擾的
in trouble 片 在困境中

反話

backhanded remark （名詞）

流行語解密！

backhanded 這個形容詞意為「諷刺挖苦的」。除 remark 外，與其固定搭配的名詞還有 compliment。Backhanded compliment = left-handed compliment 意為「諷刺挖苦的恭維話」。

這樣用就對了！

1. Joseph is always making a backhanded remark about my girlfriend.
   約瑟夫老是說我女朋友的反話。

2. Sometimes I could hear Arlene making remarks about her English teacher.
   有時我可以聽見艾蓮在說她英文老師的反話。

3. I hate to hear anyone paying me a backhanded compliment.
   我不喜歡聽到任何人對我說諷刺挖苦的恭維話。

隨口說出的話；脫口而出的話

throwaway remark （名詞）

流行語解密！

throwaway 是個形容詞，意為「隨口說出的；脫口而出的」。此外，它還意為「一次性（使用）的；拋棄式的」(= disposable)，如 throwaway razor/toothbrush/tableware（一次性 / 拋棄式刮鬍刀 / 牙刷 / 餐具）。

這樣用就對了！

1. The president's throwaway remark caused a political furor.
   總統隨口說的一句話引起一場政治騷動。

2. Linda's throwaway remarks hurt me deeply.
   琳達隨口說出的話讓我很受傷。

動一根汗毛

harm my hair on someone's head

流行語解密！

這句話也可以用 touch（觸碰）說成 touch a hair of someone's head，或是 touch a hair on someone's head，直接翻譯是觸碰一根頭髮，跟中文「動一根汗毛」意思一樣，都是說對他人造成微小的傷害。

這樣用就對了！

1. "My dear love," said the elder lady, as she folded the weeping girl in her bosom, "do you think I would harm my hair on his head?" – Oliver Twist
「親愛的，」那位年長的夫人一邊說，一邊把那個哭泣的女孩摟在懷裡，「你想我會碰他一根汗毛嗎？」--《孤雛淚》

2. If the kidnapper harms a hair on my daughter's head, I'll kill him.
如果綁匪敢動我女兒一根汗毛，我就殺了他。

Track 063

家裡沒大人
When/While the cat's away the mice will play.

流行語解密！

這句話直接翻譯是：貓不在，老鼠就作怪，或是：山中無老虎，猴子稱大王，也就是現在人常說的「家裡沒大人（小孩會作怪）」。這句經常縮略為 when/while the cat's away。

這樣用就對了！

1. Do you think it's wise to leave the children alone for so long? You know, when the cat's away.
你認為讓孩子獨處這麼長的時間行得通嗎？你知道，貓不在，老鼠就作怪。

2. The boss is away on business and the employees are so happy because while the cat's away the mice will play.
老闆出差，員工都很高興，因為山中無老虎，猴子稱大王。

接下來的事你（們）都知道了

The rest is history.

流行語解密！

這是我們生活中很常用的一句話。當你在敘述一件事或告訴人家某事時，說著說著，如果接下來的事情是大家都知道的，那麼往往以「接下來的事你（們） 都知道了」或「接下來的事大家都知道了」帶過，以避免浪費口舌。

這樣用就對了！

1. Larry and Cindy got married and the rest is history.
   賴瑞和辛蒂結婚了，接下來的事你都知道了。

2. Donald Trump won the presidency in the presidential election of 2016 and the rest is history.
   川普在 2016 年的總統選舉中當選總統，接下來的事大家都知道了。

Track 065

傻人有傻福

Fortune favors fools.

流行語解密！

這是從 Fortune favors the brave.（勇者理當走好運。）此一諺語轉換而來。還可以說 God sends fortune to fool（神把好運給了傻瓜），或是 fortune's fool，這句話不只是現在流行語，早在數百年前莎士比亞的《羅密歐與朱麗葉》中便用了一句“I am fortune's fool”，直接翻譯是好運眷顧的傻子，也就是傻人有傻福的意思。

這樣用就對了！

1. People think she's a fool to marry a dandy. After the marriage, however, her husband only loves her and is very nice to her. Isn't she a fortune's fool?
大家都說她嫁給這花花公子很傻，但是婚後她丈夫只愛她而且對她很好，她真是傻人有傻福啊。

2. I believe that fortune favors fools.
我相信傻人有傻福。

Track 066

張三李四；阿貓阿狗

every Tom, Dick, and Harry （名詞）

流行語解密！

Tom, Dick 跟 Harry 都是常見的名字，所以用來泛指張三李四，任何一個人。亦可用 any Tom, Dick, and Harry 來表示。

這樣用就對了！

1. It is not a good idea to invite every Tom, Dick, and Harry to the party.
邀請那些張三李四都來參加派對不太好。

2. Close the window or we'll have every Tom, Dick, and Harry to hear what we say.
關上窗戶，否則隨便哪個阿貓阿狗都可以聽到我們說什麼。

3. I want a qualified worker, not just any Tom, Dick, or Harry.
我需要一個適任的工人，不是隨便哪個阿貓阿狗都可以。

Chapter 4

大家都這樣說！

好屌

rock （動詞）

流行語解密！

這個字為美國口語，意為「好屌；很屌；真棒」。rock 除了當名詞有岩石的意思之外，還有搖滾的意思，如果說人 rock 就是說人家很酷很厲害，而 rock 跟中文的「很屌」一樣，跟男性性器官有關，所以用 rock 表達「很屌」是再恰當不過的了。

這樣用就對了！

1. You breezed through all your exams. You rock!
   你輕易地通過所有考試。你好屌！

2. Her new smartphone really rocks!
   她的新智慧型手機真的很屌！

3. The baseball player hit two home runs including a grand slam. He rocks!
   那位棒球選手擊出兩支全壘打，包括一支滿貫全壘打。他好屌！

★ **breeze** [briz] 名 微風／動 微風輕吹
　▶延伸片語：**breeze through** 輕鬆通過（考試）

★ **include** [ɪnˋklud] 動 包含

★ **slam** [slæm] 動 打出去

超

super（副詞）

流行語解密！

「超」這個字從日本流行到台灣，成為現今最夯的流行語之一，講話時不「超」一下好像會怎樣一樣，如「我超喜歡」、「他超幼稚」、「這個東西超可愛」。有趣的是，台灣人超愛「超」的，而強國人民則超喜歡用「特」這個字來加強語氣，異曲同工。super 原本只當形容詞用（名詞用法在此略過），意為「極好的，超棒的」，如 That was a super party.（那是一場超棒的派對），但這用法已過時。super 的副詞用法最近幾年才廣為流行，意為「極為；非常；超」（extremely, very, really, so）。這一用法起源於南加州，所以一開始被稱為 SoCal English（SoCal 為 Southern California 的縮寫），但短短幾年間即流行於全美（CNN 記者和主播經常將 super 掛在嘴邊，可見一斑）、甚至北美以外的國家。然而，必須注意的是，截至目前，當副詞用的 super，都是放在形容詞前面來修飾形容詞，加強該形容詞的語氣，並無修飾動詞或其他副詞的用法。

這樣用就對了！

1. Today's supermodels are super thin.
   現今的超模都超瘦的。
2. I was super hungry when I got home last night.
   昨晚回家時我超餓的。
3. When Bill got a shiny new bike for his birthday, he was super stoked.
   比爾生日得到一台全新的腳踏車，他超爽的。
4. I'm going to Taipei to hear a concert by A Pink tomorrow, and I'm super excited.
   我明天要去台北聽韓國女團 A Pink 的演唱會，我現在超爽的。

像樣的

decent（形容詞）

流行語解密！

口語上很常用「像樣的」，形容東西恰當，例如：decent dress（像樣的裙子）。decent 還有另外幾個常見的中文意思，如「正派的」、「得體的」和「體面的」。如果要形容東西合宜恰當還可以用 proper（適當的），例如：proper manner（舉止得宜）。

這樣用就對了！

1. Why don't you find a decent job?
你為什麼不找一份像樣的工作？

2. Jocelyn didn't have a decent meal for a month.
喬瑟琳一個月沒有吃一頓像樣的飯。

3. I only make friends with good decent guys.
我只跟正派的好人交朋友。

Track 070

太瞎了／很瞎／好瞎

outrageous（形容詞）

流行語解密！

舉凡耍白痴、無厘頭、無理取鬧或不按牌理出牌的行徑，都可用「太瞎了」、「好瞎」或「很瞎」來形容，與「很扯」的意思相近。在中文「很瞎」用法比較中性，但是在英文中 outrageous 不只是荒唐的意思，還多有負面的意味，有「可憎的」、「無法無天」的意思。

這樣用就對了！

1. Fiona blames me for causing her divorce. That's outrageous!
費歐娜責怪我造成她離婚。真是太瞎了！

2. Professor Lee gave his students a test to see if they were honest enough. But I think it is he who is most outrageous!
李教授對他的學生進行測驗，想要看看他們是否夠誠實。但我認為最瞎的人就是他！

3. If you're goofy and even outrageous, you can probably be pushed out from this team.
如果你耍白痴、甚至很瞎，你可能遭到這團隊的排擠。

Track 071

真是的；真不像話

honestly（副詞）

流行語解密！

honestly 這個字原意是誠實地，在生活中用到這個字也可能會是「老實說」。如果在口語中放在句首，可以表達厭惡、惱怒、驚訝等不同意的意思，就是中文的「真不像話」、「真是的」。

這樣用就對了！

1. Honestly! What a stupid thing to do!
真是的！怎麼會幹出這種蠢事！

2. Honestly! Is it necessary for you to spend so much money every month?
真不像話！你有必要每個月花這麼多錢嗎？

別鬧了

cut it out （動詞）

流行語解密！

cut it out 字面上意思是「剪斷」，但是生活中用到這句話意為「別鬧了；住手；（叫某人）停止做（你不喜歡的某事）」。這口語亦可用 cut that out 來表示，意為「別鬧了；住手；（叫某人）停止做（你不喜歡的某事）」。這句話很常在美劇中聽到，當小孩子在吵鬧時，爸媽說 cut it out 就是「別鬧了，住手」的意思。

這樣用就對了！

1. You two idiots! Cut it out and keep quiet, won't you?
   你們兩個笨蛋！別鬧了，保持安靜，好嗎？

2. The students were fighting so their teacher told them to cut it out or they would be punished severely.
   學生在打架，他們的老師要他們住手、別鬧了，否則都要受到嚴懲。

★ **punish** [ˋpʌnɪʃ] 動 處罰
 ▶延伸片語：**punish sb for...** 因……而懲罰某人
 ▶相關詞：**punishment** [ˋpʌnɪʃmənt] 名 處罰

★ **severely** [səˋvɪr] 形 嚴厲的

Track 073

門兒都沒有；想都別想；說什麼也不行；休想；免談

over my dead body （片語）

流行語解密！

over my dead body 照字面上意思是「跨過我的屍體」，也就是中文的「我死也不要……」，表達強烈的不願意。這片語亦可用 over his dead body，但通常僅用於間接引句。

這樣用就對了！

1. A: I heard that Jeff wants to go out with your sister.
   A：我聽說傑夫想要跟你妹妹交往。
   B: Over my dead body!
   B：門兒都沒有！

2. John: I'm going to take the car tonight.
   約翰：今晚我要用一下車。
   His father: Over my dead body!
   他父親：想都別想！

哪有這種好事；哪有這麼好的事

It's too good to be true.

流行語解密！

"too good to be true" 意為「好得難以置信；好得不像是真的」，通常與 be 動詞或 become, get, sound 等連綴動詞連用。根據語境不同，這片語除可表達上述積極意思外，亦可表達「哪有這麼好的事」這一消極意思。

這樣用就對了！

1. The news was too good to be true.
   這消息好得難以置信。

2. They told me I won the lottery, but it was too good to be true.
   他們告訴我我中獎了，但這好得不像是真的。

3. A: The ad says buy one get two free.
   廣告說，買一送二。
   B: No way! It's too good to be true.
   不可能！哪有這麼好的事。

4. A: John will buy us a drink tonight.
   約翰今晚要請我們喝兩杯。
   B: Wow! It's too good to be true.
   哇！哪有這種好事。

看著辦

play it by ear（動詞）

流行語解密！

「看著辦」就是隨機應變的意思。play it by ear 意思不是用耳朵玩，而是源自於音樂的典故。原意為聽過樂曲後不看樂譜僅憑記憶演奏，或是說一些人具有音樂天賦而沒有受過專業訓練，憑著耳朵聽就能演奏。後來 play it by ear 被廣泛運用，不只是在音樂上沒有譜，也可能是做事情沒有譜，也就是看著辦的意思。

這樣用就對了！

1. I'm not sure how long I'll stay in Taipei. I'll just play it by ear.
   我不確定我會在台北停留多久。我會看著辦。

2. I haven't decided what to say in the speech; I'll play it by ear.
   我還沒決定要在演講上說什麼，到時候看著辦吧。

★ **stay** [ste] 動 （短期）待在

★ **decide** [dɪˋsaɪd] 動 決定

▶延伸片語：**decide to do sth.** 決定做某事

★ **not decide yet** 還沒有決定

★ **decide on sth.** 決定某事

瘋了
lose it （動詞）

流行語解密！

這是很常聽見的口語。字面上意思是失去它，那是失去什麼呢？其實這是失去對自己的控制而開始哭、叫等等，也就是因為某個好事或是壞事而瘋掉。lose 很常用在「喪失控制」上面，例如：lose control of oneself（失去控制）、lose someone's mind（喪失心智）等等。

這樣用就對了！

1. Tom bought NT$50,000 worth of lotto ticket? He's definitely lost it.
湯姆買了五萬塊的樂透？他肯定瘋了。

2. After Randy got dumped, he virtually lost it. I think his losing it could last several months or even a few years.
藍迪被甩後簡直瘋了。我想他的這種情況可能持續好幾個月、甚至好幾年。

Track
077

不會吧
get out of here （動詞）

流行語解密！

這是在表示不相信對方所說的話，與「少來了」意思相當。字面上意思是「離開」，現在有「不可能」的意思，這句話中的 here 當作名詞，放在介系詞後面。也可以說成 get out。此外，近年來 shut up 除了是「閉嘴」，也有類似的意思，這也是美國女生常用的口頭禪之一喔！

這樣用就對了！

1. You said Mary was willing to marry you, get out of here.
   你說瑪麗願意嫁給你，不會吧！

2. You said you solved this difficult math problem on your own, get out of here.
   你說你自己解出這個困難的數學問題，少來了！

Track 078

大事不好了；代誌大條了

The fat is in the fire

流行語解密！

the fat is in the fire 字面上的意思是油脂滴到火裡面了，可能會讓肉烤焦了或是引發火災，所以是大事不妙的意思。這俗語已存在數百年之久，主要表示「大事不妙了；要出事了；闖禍了」這樣的意思。也可以說 when the fat is in the fire。

這樣用就對了！

1. Brother: Mom found out that we broke the expensive vase.
   哥哥：媽媽發現了我們打破那個貴重的花瓶。
   Sister: Uh-oh! The fat's in the fire now.
   妹妹：喔！大事不好了！

2. Holly has discovered you've been seeing her husband, so the fat's in the fire.
   荷莉已發覺妳一直在跟她先生來往，所以大事不妙了。

3. Now the fat's in the fire. The teacher is early from the meeting and will see we haven't even started to study.
   代誌大條了。老師提早開完會，一定會看到我們都還沒開始讀書。

不敢苟同

respectfully disagree +（with+ 受詞）（動詞）

流行語解密！

respectfully disagree 是一種表示不同意的禮貌性說法。另外一種很常見的用法是I beg to differ. 字面上意思是「我乞求異議。」也是一種禮貌地表達不同意見的用法。

這樣用就對了！

1. I must respectfully disagree with what you are saying.
我不敢苟同你的說法。

2. I beg to differ. Your proposal is not going to work.
我不敢苟同你的說法。你的提議無法奏效。

Track 080

天下沒有白吃的午餐

There's no such thing as a free lunch.

流行語解密！

這句亦可說成 There ain't no such thing as a free lunch.。其中 ain't 是 is not 的口語用法。

這樣用就對了！

❶ Arthur: The sales say I can get a smartphone for free!
亞瑟：這銷售員說我可以免費得到一支智慧型手機。
Shelly: There's no such thing as a free lunch.
雪莉：天下沒有白吃的午餐。

❷ Nina gave me her smartphone, but I paid NT3000 to repair it. There's no such thing as a free lunch.
妮娜把她的智慧型手機送給我，但我須花 3,000 台幣請人修理。真是天下沒有白吃的午餐。

Track 081

好漢不吃眼前虧

He who fights and runs away lives to fight another day.

流行語解密！

有時亦寫成 He who fights and runs away may live to fight another day.，而 lives to 和 may live to 之前經常加逗點。to live to do something 意為「活到做……」、「活得夠久而得以做某事」，例如：I will live to see Apple roll out iPhone 20.（我會活到見證蘋果推出 iPhone 20）。

這樣用就對了！

❶ The school bully told Roger to meet him in the playground after school, but Roger didn't keep the appointment. When his friends called him a coward, Roger shrugged and said, "he who fights and runs away, lives (or may live) to fight another day."
那個學校惡霸要羅傑放學後去操場見他，但羅傑爽約。當羅傑的朋友叫他懦夫時，羅傑聳聳肩說：「好漢不吃眼前虧」。

叫某人吃不完兜著走；要某人好看；給某人顏色瞧瞧

have someone's guts for garters （動詞）

流行語解密！

guts 意為「內臟，腸子」，而 garter 為「吊襪帶；吊褲帶」。have someone's guts for garters 字面的意思為「把某人的腸子抽出來做吊襪帶」，也就是中文的「吃不完兜著走」的意思。

這樣用就對了！

1. If I catch you cheating again, I'll have your guts for garters.
   如果我再抓到你作弊，我就叫你吃不完兜著走。

2. The students have to hand in their homework tomorrow or else the teacher will have their guts for garters.
   學生必須在明天之前繳交他們的作業，否則老師會給他們顏色瞧瞧。

★ **cheat** [tʃit] 動 作弊，欺騙

★ **hand in** 片 繳交

別高興得太早

He who laughs last laughs longest.

流行語解密！

亦寫成 He who laughs last laughs best.，而 laughs longest 和 laughs best 之前經常加逗點。這句的原意為「最後笑的人才是真正的笑」。

這樣用就對了！

1. Keep on laughing and bragging about your current achievements, but just remember the old adage, "he who laughs last laughs longest."
   繼續笑吧、繼續自誇你目前的成就吧，但要記住這句古諺：「最後笑的人才是真正的笑。別高興得太早」。

2. Carol was bad to me, but I'll get her back. She who laughs last, laughs best.
   卡羅對我不好，但我一定會報復。別高興得太早。

Track 084

（某人）沒什麼好怕的
Someone won't bite.

流行語解密！

這是我們日常生活中經常會講的話，告訴某人他們要面對或想接觸的人沒什麼好怕的，「那個人不會咬人」。這句話很常用在面對主管的時候。

這樣用就對了！

1. Just ask Mrs. Huang. She won't bite.
   問黃女士就是了。她沒什麼好怕的。

2. I think you should talk to your boss about this. Go on, he won't bite.
   我認為你應該跟你的主管談這件事。去吧，沒關係，他這個人沒什麼好怕的。

沒什麼大不了的

It's not that big of a deal; It's no big deal; It's no biggie.

流行語解密！

這種用法常被視為非正規英文，其中 It's not that big of a deal. 中的 of 也不常在正規英文中出現，一般只要説 big deal 就好了，但是近年來「形容詞＋ of a ＋名詞」這種用法越來越常見。這幾種説法的正規用法都是 It's not a big deal. 另外一種很常見的用法是 What's the big deal? 這句話是「這有什麼了不起」的意思。

這樣用就對了！

1. I know speaking in front of a large audience will make you nervous. But stop freaking out! It's not that big of a deal.
我知道在一大群觀眾前面演講會讓你緊張。但別緊張了！沒什麼大不了的。

2. Don't worry. It's no big deal to meet your girlfriend's parents. No problem. It's actually no biggie.
別擔心。見你女友的父母親沒什麼大不了的。沒問題。真的，沒什麼大不了的。

3. It's no biggie for me to walk to work. I'm used to it.
對我來說，走路上班沒什麼大不了的。我習慣了。

GG 了

You're toast!

流行語解密！

這種用法很常在加拿大的英文中見到。雖然例句都用驚嘆號，但使用句號也可以。如果主詞是具體的東西，則是「被毀壞」的意思。類似的用法還有：be screwed。中文裡 GG 是線上遊戲中，遊戲結束會出現的 good game，後來衍生出「遊戲結束」、「完蛋了」的意思，也會說「你就 G 了」是「你就完蛋了」的意思。

這樣用就對了！

1. Oops, I'm toast!
   糟了，我 GG 了！

2. My homework is toast!
   我的功課完蛋了！

3. I'm not toast anymore!
   我有救了！

才怪；個頭

my foot（感嘆詞）

流行語解密！

這是口語上非正式的用法，亦可用 my arse（英） 來表示，但 arse 是屁股的意思，此為粗話，少用為妙。

這樣用就對了！

1. "She's an outstanding singer."
   她是傑出的歌手。
   "Outstanding my foot!"
   傑出才怪！

2. "Mom is too busy to speak to you."
   媽媽忙得沒時間跟你講話。
   "Busy, my foot! Give her the phone."
   忙？忙個頭！把電話拿給她。

★ **outstanding** [ˋaʊtˋstændɪŋ] 形 突出的，傑出的

★ **arse** [ˋars] 名 屁股

▶延伸片語：**arse about/around** 片 愚蠢舉動

說得跟真的一樣；說得好像真的一樣；說得倒好聽

famous last words（名詞）

流行語解密！

famous last words 這個片語首次出現在 1920 年代。除了用作本文的比喻意思外，它亦經常被用作字面意思，即名人臨終遺言或世界知名人物人生最後所說的話，包括蘋果公司已故創辦人賈伯斯 (Steve Jobs) 臨終前所說的"Oh wow. Oh wow. Oh wow"以及美國著名小說家、諾貝爾文學獎得主海明威 (Ernest Hemingway) 自殺前對他妻子瑪麗所說的"Goodnight my kitten."（晚安，我的小貓）。

這樣用就對了！

1. Jack: I think I should tell my wife we went to nightclub last night.
傑克：我想我應該告訴我太太，我們昨晚上夜店。
John: Famous last words.
約翰：說得好像真的一樣。

2. Elvis Presley's famous last words were "I'm going to the bathroom to read."
歌壇天王「貓王」臨終前的最後一句話是「我要去廁所看書。」

Track 089

那個什麼東西；那個叫什麼的東西

whatchamacallit

[ˋhwɑtʃəməˏkɔlɪt]（名詞）

流行語解密！

日常生活中經常會因一時忘記而突然叫不出某樣東西的名字（也可能是不知道該東西的名稱），只好用「那個什麼東西」或「那個叫什麼的東西」來帶過。「那個什麼東西」或「那個叫什麼的東西」的英文口語就叫做 whatchamacallit，是從 “what you may call it” 衍生而來。

這樣用就對了！

1. You've broken the whatchamacallit on my computer.
你把我電腦上那個什麼東西弄壞了。

2. Owen: “Hey, Paula, hand me the- the- you know, the whatchamacallit.”
歐文：「嗨，寶拉，請把那個、那個、那個叫什麼的東西遞給我。」
Paula: “The what?”
寶拉：「什麼跟什麼？」

行行好
Be an angel.

流行語解密！

angel 在口語中意為「天使般的人；大好人 (a very kind/nice person)」。如果說 You're an angel. 意思是說「你人真好」。相反的，be no angel 則是指某人犯錯或是有不好的行為。

這樣用就對了！

1. Be an angel and get me a cup of coffee.
   行行好，給我拿杯咖啡。
2. Be an angel and lend me some cash.
   請行行好借我一些錢。

Track 091

你嘛幫幫忙
Give me a break!

流行語解密！

亦寫成或唸成 "Gimme a break!" 。依照前後文，這句話可能有許多意思，可能是表達不認同，例如："He is the best employee in the company." （他是這家公司最好的員工。）／Give me a break. He made us in trouble times after time.（你嘛幫幫忙，他一次又一次地找我們麻煩好嗎？）或是要他人別來煩，例如：You asked me to go shopping again and again. Give me a break! I want to have a rest.（你老是要我陪你逛街，你嘛幫幫忙，我想要休息一下。）

這樣用就對了！

❶ Don't go on and on. Give me a break!
不要這樣沒完沒了地下去。你嘛幫幫忙！

❷ You're going to run for President? Give me a break!
你要競選總統嗎？你嘛幫幫忙！

Track 092

少來這一套
Don't patronize me.

流行語解密！

動詞 patronize 在此意為「（說話或行為）表現出高人一等的姿態；以高人一等的態度對待」。Don't patronize me. 也有「不要自以為是」的意味。

這樣用就對了！

❶ And if you're a very good boy for the doctor, you might even get a lollipop!
如果你乖乖聽醫生的話，你可能還有棒棒糖吃！
Mom, I'm fifteen. Don't patronize me!
媽，我 15 歲了。少來這一套！

❷ Don't patronize me; I know just as much about the scandal as you do.
少來這一套；我對這一醜聞知道的並不比你少。

你把我當成什麼人
What do you take me for?

流行語解密！

這句話中的 take 是「當成」的意思，take...for 還有一個很常見的片語，take it for granted（視為理所當然）。What do you take me for? 亦可用 What sort of person do you think I am? 來表示，這相當於說 I am not that sort/type of person.（我不是那種人）。

這樣用就對了！

1. Of course I didn't tell Mary your secret. What do you take me for?
   我當然沒有把你的秘密告訴瑪麗，你把我當成什麼人？

2. I will surely help you. What do you take me for?
   我當然會幫你，你把我看作什麼人？

Track 094

受夠了
have had enough （動詞）；have had it （動詞）

流行語解密！

若使用 have had enough，其後往往接 of something ／ someone 來表示受夠了某事／某人，例如：I have had enough of you.（我受夠你了！）這句話也可以說 I am fed up with you. 如果說 Enough is enough.（夠了就是夠了。）這句話用來表達更強烈的「受夠了」。

這樣用就對了！

1 I'm leaving. I've had enough of all your nonsense!
我要走了。我受夠了你的連篇廢話！

2 I've had enough of work today. I think I'll take a day off tomorrow.
我受夠了今天的工作。我想明天休一天假。

3 Paul often makes me run errands for him. I've had it! It's too much!
保羅經常要我為他跑腿。我受夠了！他太超過了！

Track 095

發發慈悲

have a heart （動詞）

流行語解密！

「發發慈悲」和「拜託做做好事」都是常用的口語或流行語，都可用 have a heart 來表示。

這樣用就對了！

1 Have a heart! I can't pay you back until three months later.
發發慈悲吧！錢三個月後我才能還你。

2 Have a heart! Don't be always borrowing money from me.
行行好吧！別老是向我借錢。

3 Have a heart! Don't call me at midnight.
拜託做做好事！別三更半夜打電話給我。

隨便你

your call; whatever; It's up to you.

流行語解密！

whatever 在口語中經常被縮略為 whatev。(It's) your call 和 It's up to you 其實就是表示「由你來決定」的意思，call 在此意為「決定」(= decision)。

這樣用就對了！

1. John: Do you wanna get spaghetti or pizza tonight?
   約翰：妳今晚想吃義大利麵還是披薩呢？
   Mary: Your call!
   瑪麗：隨便你！

2. Nobody can make this decision for you - it's your call.
   沒有人能為你做這個決定 – 這要由你來決定。

3. A：Do you want me to share this with you?
   A：你要我跟你分享這個嗎？
   B：Whatever!
   B：隨便你！

4. Are you sure you don't wanna go to the concert with me tonight? Whatever! It's up to you! Just make the call!
   你確定今晚不想跟我去聽音樂會嗎？隨便你！聽你的！就做個決定吧！

就是說嘛
Tell me about it.

流行語解密！

這是一句很常用的口語，字面上意思是「告訴我這件事吧！」但是依照前後文或是語氣，可以表示同意或附和別人的說法，即「我有同感」、「一點沒錯」、「可不是嗎」的意思。

這樣用就對了！

1. Tom: Man, what a pleasant day today!
老兄，今天天氣真是宜人啊！
Tim: Tell me about it.
就是說嘛！

2. A: The street is very crowded on the eve of Chinese Lunar New Year.
這條街在農曆新年除夕都會擠得水洩不通。
B: Tell me about it.
可不是嗎？

Track 098

過去的事就讓它過去吧
Let bygones be bygones.

流行語解密！

bygone 在這邊是當名詞，是「過去」的意思。這英文也就是「盡棄前嫌」、「既往不咎」的意思。

這樣用就對了！

1. Despite the fact that her father treats her very badly, she has decided to let bygones be bygones and take care of him when he is too old.
儘管她父親對她很不好，但她已決定過去的事就讓它過去，在他垂垂老矣時照顧他。

2. Fiona held a grudge against her teacher for a long time, but she finally decided to let bygones be bygones.
費歐娜對她老師懷恨已久，但她最後決定盡棄前嫌。

★ **despite the fact that...** 片 儘管

★ **grudge** [ˋgrʌdʒ] 動 憎恨 名 怨恨

三三兩兩

in/by dribs and drabs （片語）

流行語解密！

這成語亦可表示「零零碎碎；點點滴滴」的意思。其中 drib 是一點點的意思，drab 則是單調的意思。

這樣用就對了！

1. The guests arrived in dribs and drabs.
   賓客三三兩兩地到來。

2. I learn Japanese in dribs and drabs.
   我零零星星的學了點日文。

3. The work had been coming in by dribs and drabs for several years.
   幾年來，接到的工作都是零零碎碎的。

Chapter 5

你也跟風打卡了嗎？

打臉

slap in the face （動詞）

流行語解密！

英文中 slap in the face 可以當作打巴掌的意思，近年來在網路上流行這詞，意思是找出別人誤會的事實，藉此讓他丟臉，有時候還會加上一個「神」變成「神打臉」，或是「（打臉打到）臉腫腫的」，意思都是因為被找出錯以為的事情而非常難為情。

這樣用就對了！

1. The president who declared his honesty was slapped in the face as the journalist found the evidence of his bribery.
   記者找到賄選的證據後，那名宣稱耿直的總統被神打臉了。

2. He always claims his assignment is perfect. But the teacher slapped in his face by indicating his mistakes.
   他總是說他的作業是完美的。但是老師指出他的錯誤真的是打臉他了。

Track 101

已讀不回

MIA (missing in action), friendly fade, ghost

流行語解密！

不管是 MIA, ghost 或是 friendly fade 都是默默神隱的意思，在網路上這意思就是不想要回覆你的訊息，也就是「已讀不回」。

這樣用就對了！

1. He is into his school sister, but she friendly fades.
他很喜歡那學妹，可是那學妹對他已讀不回。

2. My classmate keeps sending me messages even though I have ghosted him.
我都已經已讀不回了，我同學還一直傳訊息給我。

Track 102

（臉書）打卡

check in （動詞）

流行語解密！

打卡也可以是名詞，英文為 check-in。另外 check-in 除了打卡，還很常用在機場或是飯店報到，而機場的報到櫃台就是叫 check-in counter。

這樣用就對了！

1. You checked-in in Taipei last night, but now you are saying you are in New York?
你昨晚還在台北打卡，現在跟我說你人在紐約？

2. Check-in has become a part of my life.
打卡已成為我生活的一部份。

跟風

jump/ climb on the bandwagon（動詞）

流行語解密！

跟風是說人跟隨著流行，但是往往有負面的意含，指人沒有自己的判斷能力就盲目地追流行，在英文會用 jump/climb on the bandwagon 表示跟風。bandwagon 本來是指遊行時的樂隊車，在遊行中往往扮演著帶領隊伍的角色，後來也衍生出「流行」的意思，而 jump/climb on the bandwagon 直譯是「跳上／爬上樂隊車」，就是跟上流行、趕時髦、或是跟風的意思了。

這樣用就對了！

1. People jump on the bandwagon of buying this kind of milk tea though there is nothing special in it.
人們跟風去買了這款奶茶，雖然這奶茶根本沒有什麼特別的。

2. I don't climb on the bandwagon of hair-coloring because my hair color suits me well.
我不會跟風染頭髮，因為我本來的髮色就很適合我了。

★ **special** [ˋspɛʃəl] 形 特別的

★ **suit** [sut] 動 適合

不穿內褲

go commando （動詞）

流行語解密！

go commando 的意思是「穿褲子但不穿內褲」，可指男性和女性。據稱，這個片語來自英國皇家陸戰隊突擊隊 (Royal Marine Commandos)，其中 commando（複數為 commandos 或 commandoes）意為「突擊（部）隊；突擊隊員」。為何 go + commando 的意思是「穿褲子但不穿內褲」呢？迄今仍是個謎。有一項說法或解釋是這樣的：由於突擊隊必須深入敵人領土進行突擊行動，他們可能發現內褲讓他們不舒服且會限制行動，或者內急時浪費太多時間脫內褲，所以經常不穿內褲出任務。

這樣用就對了！

1. Amy usually goes commando.
   艾美經常不穿內褲出門。

2. He went commando yesterday.
   昨天他沒穿內褲就出門。

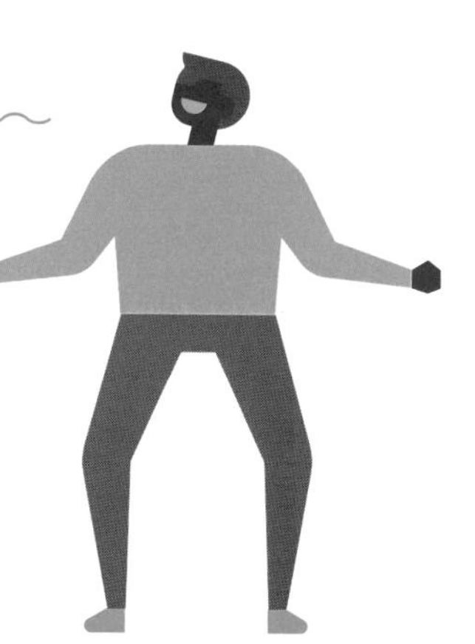

★ **royal** [ˋrɔɪəl] 形 皇家的

★ **marine** [məˋrin] 形 航海的

撞衫

wear the same kind of dress/clothes/clothing as someone （動詞）

流行語解密！

這個流行語亦可用 to dress in the same style and color 來表示。網路上流傳「撞衫」的英文是 clash with an outfit，非也！這是以訛傳訛的說法。clash with an outfit 的意思是「衣服不搭配」。同樣地，英文還有 outfit clash 的說法，但這一用語的意思也是「衣服不搭配」，不是「撞衫」，例如：Outfit clashes are taboo to celebs.（名流忌諱穿衣服不搭配）。

這樣用就對了！

1. When the movie star was walking on the red carpet, she found she happened to be wearing the same kind of dress as others.
   那影星走紅地毯時發現她與其他人撞衫了。

2. At the award-giving party, the two supermodels happened to be dressed in the same style and color.
   在頒獎晚會上，這兩位超模撞衫了。

3. His T-shirt clashed with his shorts.
   他的 T 恤和短褲不相配。

★ **carpet** [ˋkɑrpɪt] 名 地毯／動 鋪地毯

★ **happen to** 片 剛好

你的拉鍊沒拉

Your fly is open. / Your fly is undone.

流行語解密！

fly 在此當名詞用，意為「褲子上的鈕扣或拉鍊的遮布或遮蓋」。相關的片語還有 inside out，是用來說人衣服裡外穿反了，另外一種很尷尬的情況是 one the wrong foot ／ hand，是說人的手套、鞋襪等穿錯邊了。

這樣用就對了！

1. His fly is open.
   他的拉鍊沒拉。

1. Your brother's fly is undone.
   你兄弟的拉鍊沒拉。

1. The girl's T-shirt is inside out. Should I tell her?
   那女孩的衣服穿反了，我該告訴她嗎？

Track 107

（衣服）省布料

scantily clad（形容詞）/ show too much skin （動詞）

流行語解密！

流行用語的「省布料」意思是「穿著暴露」，scantily clad 亦意為「衣著單薄的」（= underclothed）。其中 scantily 是「吝嗇的」意思，clad 則是「穿……覆蓋著」。

這樣用就對了！

1. How scantily clad your sister is!
   你妹妹穿得好暴露啊！

2. Martha is always showing too much skin.
   瑪莎老是穿著暴露。

3. People who are scantily clad in winter are more likely to get sick.
   冬天衣著單薄的人，生病的風險較高。

Track 108

眼皮跳

eyelid twitches

流行語解密！

twitch 可當（及物或不及物）動詞和（可數）名詞用，意為（身體某個部分）抽動，抽搐。其實在不同文化中，左眼皮跟右眼皮跳動有不同的迷信，在華人世界有種說法是左跳財右跳災，但是在印度等其他文化中，左邊是好運而右邊是災難。所以要說眼皮跳時，要注意不同的文化風俗喔！

這樣用就對了！

1. My eyelid's twitching.
我的眼皮在跳。

2. I believe that left eyelid twitches indicate fortune.
我相信左眼跳財。

Track 109

割雙眼皮

double eyelid surgery （名詞）

流行語解密！

lid 是蓋子的意思，所以 eyelid 是眼睛的蓋子，也就是眼皮囉！單眼皮和雙眼皮的英文分別為 single eyelid 和 double eyelid。割雙眼皮是在韓國等東亞地區比較常見，所以有種稱呼是 East Asian blepharoplasty。而 surgery 則是外科手術的意思，很常用在各種外科整形手術（plastic surgery）上。

這樣用就對了！

1. Double eyelid surgery is the most common in South Korea.
割雙眼皮在南韓很常見。

2. I want to go to Korea to have double eyelid surgery.
我想要去韓國割雙眼皮。

3. There are many double eyelid surgery clinics in that country.
那個國家有許多割雙眼皮診所。

拉皮

facelift（名詞）

流行語解密！

這個字是 face（臉）＋ lift（舉起），也就是俗稱的拉皮。也可以寫作 face-lift 或是 face lift。這個字亦意為建築物的「翻修；整修」。

這樣用就對了！

1. I had a facelift three months ago.
   我三個月前做了拉皮。

2. There seems to be no such thing as a facelift without surgery.
   目前似乎還沒有不動手術的拉皮。

Track 111

肉毒桿菌

Botox（名詞）

流行語解密！

一種醫學美容產品，透過微針注射在臉部、小腿和手臂等部位以達到瘦面、瘦腿和撫平皺紋等效果，使皮膚看起來更光滑年輕。注射肉毒桿菌是 inject Botox 或是 application of Botox。施打肉毒桿菌常常是為了要消除魚尾紋等皺紋，但是魚尾紋的英文跟中文不一樣，是 crow's feet。

這樣用就對了！

1. An application of Botox only lasts about three or four months.
肉毒桿菌施打一次只維持三或四個月。

2. The market for Botox is growing rapidly in Taiwan.
台灣的肉毒桿菌市場急速增長。

Track 112

醫美

aesthetic medicine （名詞）

流行語解密！

醫美為醫學美容的簡稱。aesthetic medicine 與 cosmetic/plastic surgery（整形外科）並不相同；同樣地，doctor of aesthetic medicine（醫美醫生）亦有別於 cosmetic/plastic surgeon（整形外科醫生），簡單來說，醫美是整型外科的一部分，而整型外科還包含顏面傷患等整形。

這樣用就對了！

1. Bruce is a doctor of aesthetic medicine.
布魯斯是醫美醫生。

2. Dr. White is a member of the American Academy of Aesthetic Medicine (AAAM).
懷特醫生是美國醫美學會的會員。

笑一個

say cheese （動詞）

流行語解密！

就像拍照時中文會說「西瓜甜不甜」，英文中常用來對擺好姿勢準備照相的人說 say cheese，因為說 cheese 這個字時，口型似微笑。

這樣用就對了！

1. Photographers usually tell you to say cheese before you get your picture taken.
   攝影師在拍照之前經常會叫你笑一個。

2. Photographer: Say cheese!
   攝影師：笑一個！
   Lori, Dave, Jessica, and Benjamin, cheese!
   蘿莉、戴夫、潔西卡和班傑明，Cheese!

Track 114

自拍

selfie （名詞）

流行語解密！

自拍指的是用手機或是數位相機幫自己拍照，通常字拍照會放在網路平台上。在英文中 selfie 也是「自拍照」。自拍的動作，英文叫做 to take a selfie / to take selfies。此外，自拍常常會用自拍棒，讓照片的視野比較廣，而自拍棒就是 selfie stick。

這樣用就對了！

1. Joanne wanted to show me her selfies.
瓊安想要讓我看她的自拍照。

2. Dude, I saw you take a selfie last night!
哥們，昨晚我看見你自拍！

Track 115

叫我一聲；喊我一聲

give me a shout （動詞）

流行語解密！

give me a shout 中的 me，可視情況改為適當的人稱受詞，如「叫他 / 她一聲」就是 give him/her a shout。另外有一個很像的片語是 give someone a shout-out，但是意思並不一樣，這是在電視訪談等場合時，非正式的表示感謝之意的意思，例如：I want to give my teacher a shout-out for inspiring me so much.（我要感謝我的老師啟發我很多事情。）

這樣用就對了！

1. Just give me a shout if you have any questions.
如果你有任何問題，就叫我一聲。

2. Give me a shout when it's ready.
準備好後喊我一聲。

自由行

independent tour/travel（名詞）

流行語解密！

旅遊方式相似的「自助旅行」叫做 backpacking（背包客：backpacker)。跟團旅行有好幾種說法，包括 escorted tour, group tour, guided tour, escorted group tour, guided group tour 等。近年來很流行的獨自旅行，英文叫做「solo traveling」，其中 solo 是一個人的意思。

這樣用就對了！

1. I prefer independent tours to escorted tours.
   我喜歡自由行更勝於跟團旅行。

2. North Korea independent tours are not allowed.
   北韓不允許自由行。

Track 117

三寸不爛之舌

a silver tongue（名詞）

流行語解密！

silver tongue 是說人表達流利、擅長說服他人。亦可用形容詞 silver-tongued 來表達相同的意思。至於中文與其同義的成語還有「如簧之舌」、「鼓舌如簧」、「能言善道」等。

這樣用就對了！

❶ I hope you've not allowed yourself to be persuaded by Rachel's silver tongue.
我希望你沒被瑞秋的三寸不爛之舌所說動。

❷ Jimmy has a sliver tongue.
= Jimmy is silver-tongued.
吉米能言善道。

Track 118

吃螺絲

trip over one's own tongue（動詞）

流行語解密！

有人認為「吃螺絲」的英文就是 tongue-tied，這是不對的，因為 tongue-tied 意為「張口結舌的；說不出話的」，而「吃螺絲」的意思是咬字、口齒或說話不清，兩者自是不能等量齊觀。至於說起來或念起來拗口的東西，則叫做 a tongue twister，這個詞亦意為「繞口令」。

這樣用就對了！

❶ Most people trip over their own tongues when they say aboriginal names.
大多數人在念原住民的名字時都會吃螺絲。

❷ The news anchorwoman is always tripping over her own tongue.
這位女新聞主播老是吃螺絲。

❸ This name is a tongue twister.
這個名字真難念。

黃色笑話
off-color joke（名詞）

流行語解密！

off-color joke 主要指「黃色笑話」，但暴力、種族歧視及其他冒犯性話題的笑話亦叫做 off-color joke。講黃色笑話的動詞可以用 crack 或是 make。

這樣用就對了！

1. The men all sat there drinking beer and cracking off-color jokes.
   男人們全都坐在那兒喝著啤酒，說著黃色笑話。

2. The boss is always making off-color jokes.
   老闆老是說葷笑話。

Track 120

心動不如馬上行動；坐而言不如起而行
Actions speak louder than words.

流行語解密！

這句英文亦可表達「聽其言不如觀其行」的意思。

這樣用就對了！

1. Actions speak louder than words. Let’s go to the movies tonight.
   心動不如馬上行動。今晚去看電影吧。

2 You keep saying that you'll do your best to clean the bedroom. Remember that actions speak louder than words.
你不斷說你會盡全力打掃臥房。記得：坐而言不如起而行。

3 The government is good at making promises but as we all know, actions speak louder than words.
政府很擅長做承諾，但眾所周知，聽其言不如觀其行。

Track 121

仆街

planking（名詞）; plank（動詞）

流行語解密！

仆街之所以叫做 planking，乃因仆街者全身筆直，面朝下，「仆倒」在著名景點、甚至匪夷所思的地方，身體僵硬如（厚）木板（plank)。當然啦，仆街之後還要拍照並將照片上傳到網路與粉絲分享才算完成整個仆街過程。仆街的人或仆街客叫做 planker。

這樣用就對了！

1 A man is planking on a motorcycle.
一名男子正仆街在機車上。

2 Three women planked in the tree.
三名女子在樹上仆街。

早操；健身操

one's daily dozen （名詞）

流行語解密！

daily 是每天的，dozen 本來是「一打」的意思，但是用在 daily dozen 這用法上，通常指每天做的早操或健身操。要注意這是比較口語化的用法喔！

這樣用就對了！

1. Doing your daily dozen is good for your health.
你知道做健身操有益健康。

2. My grandma has been feeling much better since she started doing her daily dozen.
自從開始做早操以來，我奶奶身體好多了。

跑腿

run an errand / run errands （動詞）

流行語解密！

errand 是差事的意思。這片語後面往往接 for someone 來表示為某人跑腿；我們亦可用 do an errand 或 do errands 來表達相同的意思。至於跑腿的人，尤其是公司或組織中職司跑腿、打雜的小職員或小弟小妹，英文叫做 gofer。

這樣用就對了！

❶ She's out running errands for her mother.
她外出為她媽媽跑腿。

❷ I have no time to do errands for you.
我沒有時間為你跑腿。

❸ I sent my gofer for coffee half an hour ago. If he doesn't get back soon, I'm dropping his health care benefits!
我半小時前派我跑腿打雜的職員去買咖啡。如果他不馬上回來，我將取消他的健保福利！

Track 124

尬車；飆車

drag, race （動詞）

流行語解密！

尬車的名詞為 drag race 或 drag racing。其中 drag race 比較常指的是短距離的直線加速賽。

這樣用就對了！

❶ Bill and Tony wanted to drag at midnight.
比爾和東尼想要午夜尬車。

❷ Let's race!
我們來尬車吧！

❸ Let's go to a drag race.
我們去看尬車。

開夜車

all-nighter（名詞）；pull an all-nighter（動詞）；burn the midnight oil（動詞）

流行語解密！

開夜車在口語上是熬夜的意思，這與 night owl（夜貓子）並不相同。注意：all-nighter 前面的動詞慣用 pull。

這樣用就對了！

1. We pulled an all-nighter to finish the report.
   我們開夜車來完成報告。

2. I pulled an all-nighter to study for my physics exam.
   我開夜車 K 書準備物理考試。

3. A lot of college students pull all-nighters for exams.
   許多大學生為考試開夜車。

Track 126

蠟燭兩頭燒

burn the candle at both ends（動詞）

流行語解密！

蠟燭兩頭燒是指白天忙碌，晚上又睡得遲，或是同時身兼多職。

這樣用就對了！

1. No wonder Anna is ill. She has been burning the candle at both ends for a long time.
難怪安娜生病了。她長期蠟燭兩頭燒。

2. He has been burning the candle at both ends with his work and his studies.
為了兼顧工作和學業，他一直蠟燭兩頭燒。

Track 127

酒駕

drunk driving; drunken driving; drink driving（名詞）

流行語解密！

drink driving 為英國特有的用法。在法律上，酒後駕車的正式用語並非 drunk/drunken driving，而是 DWI (driving while intoxicated) – intoxicated 意為「（酒）醉的；陶醉的」。除了 DWI 之外，還有另一個表示「酒後駕車」的用語亦不時被使用，那就是 DUI (driving under the influence)。

這樣用就對了！

1. He was arrested for/charged with drunk driving.
他因酒駕被捕 / 他被控酒駕。

2. There's no excuse for drunk driving.
酒駕沒有什麼理由可說。

吃霸王餐；白吃白喝

dine and dash （動詞）

流行語解密！

dine and dash 的過去式和過去分詞為 dined and dashed。除當動詞外，dine and dash 亦可當名詞用。若將這三個字以連字號連接，則可當形容詞用，如 a dine-and-dash couple（吃霸王餐的情侶）；a dine-and-dash customer（白吃白喝的顧客）。

目前已知這片語還有幾個同義詞，包括 dine and ditch, dine and run, chew and screw, run the check 及 mash and dash 等。值得一提的是，中文對於吃霸王餐還有一個更通俗的稱呼，那就是「跑單」。對照上述的英文用語，跑單不就是 run the check 的直譯嗎！這裡的 check 意為「（餐廳的）帳單」。

這樣用就對了！

1. A couple dined and dashed at an upscale restaurant in Taipei last night but got caught one hour later.
   一對情侶昨晚在台北一家高檔餐廳吃霸王餐後逃逸，但一小時後被逮。

2. They went to the restaurant and pulled/had a dine and dash.
   他們去那家餐廳吃霸王餐。

★ **upscale** [ˋʌp͵skel] 形 高檔的

★ **customer** [ˋkʌstəmɚ]
名 1. 顧客 2. 消費者

被抓包

be busted （動詞）

流行語解密！

舉凡做壞事或做虧心事被逮到、被抓包，都可用 be busted 來表示，busted 在此為形容詞，乃俚語的「失敗的」之意。但 bust 本身除了當動詞和名詞（意為「逮捕；搜查」）之外，亦可當形容詞用，意為「壞了的；破產的」，通常與 be/go 連用，如 My computer is bust.（我的電腦壞了）；I'm surprised his company went bust after only a year in business.（他的公司只經營一年就破產 / 倒閉了，我感到驚訝）。

這樣用就對了！

1. Daniel was busted and had to confess (to) cheating in/on the exam.
   丹尼爾被抓包，只好承認考試作弊。

2. I'm busted! Now everyone knows I have a big crush on Teresa.
   我被抓包了！現在每個人都知道我暗戀泰瑞莎。

3. Amy was busted cheating on her husband after selfies revealed the hidden truth.
   在自拍照透露隱藏的真相後，艾美對她丈夫不忠的情事被抓包了。

★ **confess** [kən'fɛs] 動 承認、供認

▶ 延伸片語：**confess one's crime** 認罪

放（某人）鴿子

stand someone up （動詞）

流行語解密！

放某人鴿子是 stand someone up，也可以用被動式表示「被放鴿子」。放人家鴿子的人就是爽約的人，英文叫做 no-show。

這樣用就對了！

1. I got stood up!
   我被人放了鴿子！

2. Did Vicky stand you up yesterday?
   維琪昨天放你鴿子嗎？

3. I arranged to have a dinner with Joe, but he stood me up. He was a no-show.
   我安排跟喬吃晚餐，但他放我鴿子。他爽約了。

Track 131

搶錢；敲竹槓

rip-off（名詞）；rip off （動詞）

流行語解密！

to rip off 後面若接人當受詞，該受詞可放在 rip 或 off 之後，即 rip someone off 或 rip off someone。

這樣用就對了！

❶ A: How much did you pay for a coffee at the airport?
你在機場一杯咖啡買多少錢？
B: Three hundred NT dollars! What a rip off!
台幣 300 元！搶錢啊！

❷ Tourists are worried they'll get ripped-off.
觀光客擔心被敲竹槓。

Track 132

擺烏龍；搞烏龍

mix-up（名詞）

流行語解密！

烏龍係廣東話的慣用語；擺烏龍、搞烏龍是指一個人不小心做錯事、講錯話、認錯人等等。在足球等比賽中，球員自進己方球門、導致對方得分的球稱為「烏龍球」，英文叫做 own goal。

這樣用就對了！

❶ There was a mix-up at the company and they lost my payment.
這家公司擺了烏龍，他們弄丟了我的付款。

❷ There was a big mix-up over the reservations and we had to stay at different hotels.
旅館預訂出了大烏龍，我們不得不住在不同的旅館。

算舊帳

settle a score/ settle an old score （動詞）

流行語解密！

亦可用 settle scores 來表達完全相同的意思。這些英文成語還可表示「尋仇；報宿怨」的意思，通常與 with 連用。

這樣用就對了！

1. Cindy was eager to settle a score with Maggie.
   辛蒂急於找瑪姬算帳。

2. Challenging him was partly a matter of settling old scores.
   向他下戰帖有部分是為了報一箭之仇。

Track 134

翻舊帳；舊事重提

rake over the ashes/coals （動詞）

流行語解密！

事實上，rake over 這個片語動詞 (phrasal verb) 的意思就是「翻舊帳」，其受詞可放在 rake 和 over 之間或 over 之後，但以後者居多。

這樣用就對了！

1. There's no point in raking over the ashes - all that happened twenty years ago, and there's nothing we can do about it now.
舊事重提已沒什麼意義了 － 那一切都發生在二十年前，現在我們也無能為力了。

2. His wife always rakes over the coals of their old unpleasant things when she is angry.
他太太一生氣就會將他們之間不愉快的往事重新搬出來。

Track 135

落湯雞

a drowned rat （名詞）

流行語解密！

與 look like 構成 look like a drowned rat 這個成語，意為「全身濕透；濕得像落湯雞（尤指在大雨中被淋濕）」。

這樣用就對了！

1. My father had to fix the fences in the storm and looked like a drowned rat.
我父親必須在暴風雨中修理籬笆，他渾身濕透，像隻落湯雞。

2. Kevin had to cycle home in the rain and came in looking like a drowned rat.
凱文必須冒雨騎腳踏車回家，進門時全身濕得像隻落湯雞。

Chapter 6

你都怎麼形容他？

人生勝利組

the whole package （名詞）

流行語解密！

人生勝利組是指具有許多理想特質或特性以及眾多內在和外在優越條件的人，如才貌兼具又擁有名校高學歷的富二代。The whole package 雖亦可指事物，但通常指人，在句中往往放在 be 動詞後面當主詞補語，複數為 the whole packages。人生勝利組的對應詞為「魯蛇」（loser）。

這樣用就對了！

1. Most of us are not the whole package.
我們大多數人都不是人生勝利組。

2. Wow! Our new marketing manager is the whole package. She has a beautiful face, a fancy car, very high intelligence, and financial stability.
哇！我們新的銷售經理是人生勝利組。她人長得美、坐擁名車、聰明過人，而且財務穩定。

Track 137

暖男

caring guy （名詞）

流行語解密！

暖男是給人很溫暖感覺的男性，性格很體貼且擅長照顧別人，對家人朋友很好，且顧家又疼小孩，在外通常打扮清新平易近人。在英文會說 caring boy，其中 caring 就是「擅長照顧他人的」，所以 caring boy 就是所謂的「暖男」。

這樣用就對了！

1. Her boyfriend is such a caring boy! He gets up early to make breakfast for her every day.
   她男朋友真是個暖男！他每天早起為她準備早餐耶！

2. He is a caring boy but he is not single.
   他是個暖男，但是他已經死會了。

Track 138

工具人
errand boy（名詞）

流行語解密！

工具人通常是指男性為女性付出很多，可能早上溫馨接送，晚上貼心買宵夜，隨傳隨到，熱心處理女性電腦等問題，但是許久之後女性依然無動於衷，因為女性只是習慣有人對她好，卻沒有把付出的男性當作戀愛對象。工具人常跟公主病一起連用。在英文中的 errand boy 是指負責跑腿打雜的男孩，跟中文的工具人雷同。

這樣用就對了！

1. Don’t ask him to buy the supper for you every day. He is not an errand boy.
   不要每天都叫他買晚餐給你。他不是工具人。

2. You shouldn’t treat him like an errand boy. He is really into you.
   你不要把他當成工具人，他是真的很喜歡你。

肉腳

wuss, wussy （名詞）

流行語解密！

肉腳是台語，有很爛、很菜的意思，指的是軟弱沒有用的人。最初只有肉腳，後來又有「滷肉腳」，意思一樣，跟國語的軟腳蝦同義。wussy 是由 wimp（懦夫；軟腳蝦；懦弱的人）和 pussy（娘炮；娘娘腔）組合而成。所以，wussy 這個字的意思有「朝三暮四」、「猶豫不定」的意思。

這樣用就對了！

1. Don't be such a wuss all the time.
   別一直這麼肉腳。

2. Tom is scared to say what he is thinking. What a wuss!
   湯姆不敢說出他心裡所想的事情。真是肉腳！

Track 140

色狼

lecher （名詞）; pervert （名詞）

流行語解密！

pervert 為「性變態者」。pervert 本身是「使變形」、「使歪曲」的意思，後來隱含有「強迫、引誘性交」的意思。另外還有一個字，lecher 為「好色之徒」，兩者都是俗稱的「色狼」。口語上罵人變態或是有病也可以用 sick、wicked。

這樣用就對了！

1. Watch out for Brian! He's an infamous lecher.
小心提防布萊恩！他是個惡名昭彰的色狼。

2. Perverts are everywhere.
色狼隨處可見。

3. Women in India are always in the fear of lechers.
印度婦女總是恐懼著色狼。

Track 141

老色狼；老色鬼

goat （名詞）

流行語解密！

goat 除了山羊之外也可指好色之徒，如果要強調年紀大，可以用 old goat。這是個侮辱性用語，使用上必須謹慎小心。

這樣用就對了！

1. My boss is a goat. He usually touches my body deliberately.
我老闆是個老色狼。他經常故意碰觸我的身體。

2. His grandfather's a goat.
他祖父是個老色鬼。

3. The old goat always has tricks to draw girls' attention.
那老色鬼總是有把戲吸引女孩注意。

老番癲；老糊塗

dotard （名詞）

流行語解密！

Dotard 這個字為美式英語，英國出版的英文字典大多未收錄。不過，英國詩人暨劇作家湯瑪斯 · 蘭多夫 (Thomas Randolph) 在其 1632 年所寫的喜劇《The Jealous Lovers》中曾使用這個字。根據《韋氏詞典》(Merriam-Webster)，這個單詞首次使用是在 14 世紀，當初的意思是「傻瓜；蠢蛋；低能，弱智者」(imbecile)。根據美國有線電視新聞網 (CNN) 報導，這個字目前的使用率並不高。

然而，在北韓領導人金正恩罵美國總統川普是老番癲 (dotard) 之後，這個詞立即引起網路熱搜，成為舉世皆知的字彙。根據《韋氏詞典》，dotard 意為 "a person in his or her dotage"，其中 dotage 的意思是「衰老，年邁」，而 in one's dotage 意為「年老糊塗；年老昏聵」。

這樣用就對了！

1. Donald hated being treated as a dotard.
唐納討厭被看成老番癲。

2. Our boss is a dotard and we don't want to work for him anymore.
我們老闆是個老糊塗，我們不想再為他工作了。

小屁孩

punk（名詞）

流行語解密！

「小屁孩」這稱呼是因為在早期學齡前的兒童常光屁股、隨地大小便，後來用來指稱年少無知、幼稚、不成熟、不懂事、甚至無理取鬧的孩子。

Punk 原指「龐克」，是搖滾樂的一種分支，指 1970 年代末期服裝、髮型怪異，透過駭人的舉止和吵鬧的快節奏音樂來對抗權威的年輕世代次文化。後來在美國俚語中也會用來形容不懂事、無理取鬧的孩子或是年輕人。

這樣用就對了！

1. Your kid is a real punk.
你的孩子真是個小屁孩。

2. Don't be a punk.
別當小屁孩。

3. You little punk!
你這個小屁孩！

萌妹子；蘿莉

girly girl （名詞）

流行語解密！

蘿莉源自 1955 年出版的小說《洛麗塔》(曾被改編成電影，中文片名為《一樹梨花壓海棠》) 中的同名女主角，其劇情描寫中年男子愛上未成年少女的故事。本來蘿莉指的是未發育，尚未有第二性徵的少女，但後來「蘿莉」這個詞就被用來指清純可愛，讓人想要保護的女孩。後來蘿莉也成為一種風格，如蘿莉塔時裝 (Lolita fashion)，其風格類似古典的少女裝，包括及膝裙、蕾絲邊、絲帶、長襪、厚底鞋、精巧的裝飾物等。而萌妹子則是起源自美少女的遊戲，外觀清純甜美可愛，性格傻得可愛且溫柔體貼的女孩。在英文則會用 girly girl，girly 是形容詞，意思是女孩子的。

這樣用就對了！

1. Claire is such a girly girl because she is very innocent and she has everything in pink. Every boy wants to protect her.
克萊兒真是個萌妹子，因為她很單純，而且她的東西都是粉紅色的。所有的男孩都想要保護她。

Track 145

搶風頭

steal someone's thunder （動詞）

流行語解密！

這成語的含意包括剽竊某人的發明搶先利用、搶先做某人要做的事，亦可指用自己的言行來分散別人對另一個人的注意。另外一種說法是 steal the spotlight，其中 spotlight 是鎂光燈的意思，所以偷走鎂光燈自然就是搶了所有舞台風光，搶盡風頭的意思。

這樣用就對了！

1. Why are you coming to steal my thunder?
你來這裡搶我的風頭是什麼意思？

2. I will tell them my marriage. Don't steal my thunder.
我會告訴大家我的婚禮。不要搶我的風頭。

Track 146

寶刀未老；老當益壯

There's life in the old dog yet.

流行語解密！

這是用來對老年人做了看似力不從心的事表示驚訝，也用於老年人對他人懷疑自己已經心餘力絀表示不服。

這樣用就對了！

1. Bill: I heard your grandpa will marry a woman who is 30. He's already 85!
比爾：我聽說你爺爺要娶一名 30 歲的女子。他已經 85 歲了！
Jack: There's life in the old dog yet.
傑克：他寶刀未老。

2. I may be 90 but there's life in the old dog yet.
我也許 90 歲，但我老當益壯。

馬屁精

bootlicker; brown noser（名詞）; suck up （名詞）

流行語解密！

brown nose 或 brown noser 都有人用，均可表示馬屁精；suck up 亦寫成 suckup。

這樣用就對了！

1. Amy cozied up to her boss all the time. She's a bootlicker.
   艾美一直拍她老闆的馬屁。她是個馬屁精。

2. Mason the suck up brings an apple to the teacher every day.
   梅森這個馬屁精每天帶一個蘋果給老師吃。

3. He's such a brown noser.
   他真是個馬屁精。

★ **boot** [buːt] 名 長靴

▶ 延伸片語：**got a boot out of** 從某事當中得到樂趣
gave sb. the order of the boot
解雇某人

★ **lick** [lɪk] 動 舔

★ **cozy up** [kozɪ ʌp] 片 拍馬屁

▶ 相關詞：**cozy** 形 舒適 名 保溫罩

★ **all the time** 片 總是

人來瘋

act crazy when people visit （動詞）；act crazy in the presence of guests （動詞）

流行語解密！

人來瘋大多指小孩在客人面前或在有生人的場合表現出的一種近似胡鬧的異常興奮狀態。家中的小朋友，平常十分乖巧，可是每當客人到訪就變了個樣，吵吵鬧鬧，講都講不聽，就是標準的人來瘋。

相信很多父母都有過這樣的經歷，家裡來了客人，小孩表現得非常高興，但一開始還能正常說話吃飯，慢慢地就陷入了一種近乎瘋狂的狀態，又吵又鬧、跑來跑去、跳上跳下！客人尷尬不已，自己也不知道該怎麼讓小孩安靜下來，往往給客人留下家教不嚴的壞印象。

成年人也會人來瘋，而且毫不遜色。只是隨著年齡增長和學養加深，一般人都會慢慢收斂甚至消失。但也有人臨死都不會有多大改變，只要人來人多就愛表現引起注意，人越多越愛表現。

人來瘋沒有完全對應的英文用語，只能根據中文意思給予最貼近的翻譯，但從實際發生的狀況來看，「人來」是這項翻譯是否貼切的關鍵字。

這樣用就對了！

1. John's children are constantly acting crazy when people visit, making him feel so embarrassed.
約翰的小孩老是人來瘋，使他甚感難堪。

2. Peter's daughter acted crazy in the presence of guests yesterday so he grounded her for two weeks.
彼得的女兒昨天人來瘋，所以他就將她禁足，罰她兩週不准外出。

街頭藝人

busker （名詞）

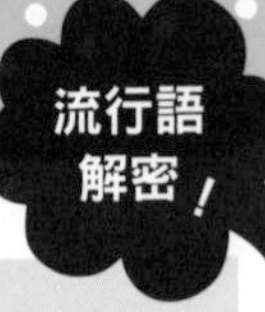

這個字衍生自動詞 busk（街頭賣藝）。亦可用 street musician 來表示。

這樣用就對了！

1. His sister has decided to be a busker.
   他姊姊已決定當街頭藝人。

2. I see a busker who plays fiddle every day.
   我每天都會看見一位街頭藝人在拉小提琴。

Track 150

難伺候

high-maintenance （形容詞）

流行語
解密！

maintenance 是維修、維護（精密的機器）的意思，high-maintenance 意思是很難維修的，用在形容人的時候，就是把人當成精細的機器一樣，很難維護保養，就是難伺候的意思。反義詞為 low-maintenance（不難伺候的）。

這樣用就對了！

1. His mom is a high-maintenance woman.
   他母親是個很難伺候的人。

❷ My boyfriend is high-maintenance.
我男朋友很難伺候。

❸ I am low-maintenance.
我不難伺候。

Track 151

比闊氣；比排場

keep up with the Joneses （動詞）

流行語解密！

Jones 是美國很常見的姓氏。“the Joneses” 並非「瓊斯一家人」，而是泛指「左鄰右舍」(the neighbors)。keep up 有「跟上……」、「保持」的意思。所以 keep up with the Joneses 是「跟上鄰居」，也就是「比排場」的意思。

這樣用就對了！

❶ Let's move if the rent is too high. We never try to keep up with the Joneses.
如果房租太高就搬家吧。我們絕對不要想比闊氣。

❷ In my neighborhood, keeping up with the Joneses has become a tradition.
在本社區，比排場已成為一種傳統。

★ **tradition** [trəˋdɪʃən] 名 傳統

▶ 延伸片語：**follow the tradition** 遵循傳統

見錢眼開；財迷心竅

have an itching palm; have itching palms （動詞）

流行語解密！

這成語原指從前人們相信手癢是進財之兆，它亦經常以當副詞用的介系詞片語 with an itching palm 型態出現。

這樣用就對了！

1. Don't trust them. They have itching palms and will certainly try to cheat you out of your prize money.
   別相信他們。他們都財迷心竅，一定會想辦法騙走你的獎金。

2. My uncle was born with an itching palm.
   我伯父天生貪財。

Track 153

揩油（的人）

mooch （動詞）,（名詞）； freeload （動詞）

流行語解密！

楷油的意思是佔人家便宜。mooch 當動詞時意為「揩油」，當名詞時意為「（愛） 揩油的人」。不過，「（愛）揩油的人」亦可用 moocher 或 freeloader 來表示。

這樣用就對了！

1. Tony's been mooching cigarettes off me for years. He's such a mooch.
多年來東尼都是向我要菸抽。他真是個愛揩油的人。

2. I can't believe you are letting Eugene stay here! All he does is eat our food, drink our beer, watch our TV and still has the nerve to ask us if we can loan him money! What a moocher!
我無法相信你竟讓尤金留在這裡！他只會吃我們的食物，喝我們的啤酒，看我們的電視，然後還敢問我們是不是可以借他錢！他真是個愛揩油的人！

3. "You're not coming over if you're going to freeload again!"
如果你想要再揩油，那你就不用來了！

4. Nelson is the biggest freeloader I've ever seen.
尼爾森是我所見過最愛揩油的人。

Track 154

手腳不乾淨

have light/sticky fingers （動詞）

流行語解密！

light-fingered 為形容詞，意為「手腳不乾淨的；有偷竊習慣的」，如 light-fingered children（有偷竊習慣的小孩）。

這樣用就對了！

1. David and his brothers all have light fingers.
大衛和他的兄弟手腳都不乾淨。

2. She has sticky fingers as many things have been stolen since she came.
她手腳不乾淨，因為她來之後許多東西遭竊。

重色輕友
hiberdating（動名詞）

流行語解密！

重色輕友就是「戀愛期間忽略其他朋友或與其他朋友中斷聯絡的情況」。hiberdating 為動名詞，這個字是由 hibernate（冬眠）和 dating（約會）組合而成，動詞為 hiberdate，至於陷入熱戀而重色輕友的人，叫做 hiberdater。在中國大陸，「重色輕友」又叫做「有異性沒人性」，顯然有異曲同工之妙。

這樣用就對了！

1. I haven't seen or heard from Michelle since she started hiberdating Allen four months ago.
自從四個月前蜜雪兒跟艾倫交往以來，我就一直沒有見到她或接獲她的消息。

2. Emma and Steve have been hiberdating for almost one year.
艾瑪和史提夫熱戀近一年來一直重色輕友。

Track 156

吃豆腐；毛手毛腳
handsy（形容詞）

流行語解密！

handsy 是用「不恰當的」、「不被接受的」方式接觸他人，也就是吃人家豆腐或是毛手毛腳的。目前大多數字典都還未收錄這個字。

這樣用就對了！

1. Honey, watch out for my Uncle Jack. He's very handsy with babes.
   親愛的，要提防我的傑克叔叔。他很喜歡吃美眉的豆腐。

2. Be careful on your date with Tony tonight because I have heard he is very handsy with the ladies.
   今晚跟東尼約會要小心，因為我聽說他對女生都會毛手毛腳。

Track 157

夜店咖

club rat （名詞）

流行語解密！

「夜店」叫做 club 或 nightclub；「上夜店」叫做 go to clubs/nightclubs, go clubbing，後者為美國俚語。

這樣用就對了！

1. Molly goes to clubs almost every night. She's a total club rat.
   茉莉幾乎每晚上夜店。她十足是個夜店咖。

2. Donna always hangs out at the club. There are many club rats like her.
   唐娜總是泡在夜店裡。現在有許多像她這樣的夜店咖。

★ **rat** [ræt] 名 老鼠

夜貓子

night owl （名詞）

流行語解密！

這與 all-nighter（開夜車；通宵 K 書） 並不相同。夜貓子是沒有在忙也是習慣性晚睡。night owl 是夜鷹的意思。

這樣用就對了！

1. Most kids these days are night owls.
現今大多數小孩都是夜貓子。

2. Teresa and her hubby are both night owls.
泰瑞莎和她先生都是夜貓子。

Track 159

重口味

intense（形容詞）

流行語解密！

重口味原指飲食方面喜愛鹹、辣等較重味道的東西，與清淡口味的意思相反，後來引伸為形容喜愛比較刺激的東西，如恐怖、暴力、血腥、色情等；換言之，一般人無法接受的事物或感到厭惡的事物，有些人卻非常欣賞或喜歡，就是重口味。intense 是「強烈的」、「極度的」的意思，衍生為「重口味」。

這樣用就對了！

1. The formula One race is kind of intense.
一號方程式賽車有點重口味。

❷ The (teaser) trailer for this new movie is quite intense.
這部新電影的預告片相當重口味。

❸ Quite a few local Taiwanese dramas are fairly intense.
許多台灣本土劇相當重口味。

★ **teaser** [tisɚ] 名 （長度較短的）廣告宣傳預告

★ **trailer** [ˋtrelɚ] 名 （電影）預告片

Track 160

名聲臭了；名譽掃地

Someone's name is mud.（成語）

流行語解密！

Someone's name is mud 這成語的出處有幾種不同的說法，但一般大多認為源自一位名叫 Samuel Mudd 的美國醫生。Dr. Mudd 因幫 1865 年刺殺林肯總統的兇手 John Wilkes Booth 接骨而被判同謀罪，因此名聲掃地。

這樣用就對了！

❶ His name's mud in the school after what happened yesterday.
昨天的事情發生之後，他在學校的名聲就臭了。

❷ If any student is caught cheating, his name will be mud.
倘若有任何學生被抓到作弊，他的名譽就掃地了。

牛牽到北京還是牛；江山易改，本性難移

A leopard doesn't/can't change its spots.

流行語解密！

這句亦可說成 "A leopard never changes its spots."。其中 leopard 是花豹，所以這句話直譯是「花豹不會改變牠的斑點」，也就是本性難移的意思。

這樣用就對了！

1. I doubt very much that marriage will change Edward for the better. A leopard doesn't change its spots.
   我非常懷疑婚姻會使愛德華變好。牛牽到北京還是牛。

2. It's not surprising that he was sentenced to five years in prison again, because a leopard never changes its spots.
   他再度被判入獄五年並不令人驚訝，因為江山易改，本性難移。

★ **leopard** [ˋlɛpɚd] 名 豹
★ **sentence** [ˋsɛntəns] 動 判決／ 名 句子、判決
★ **prison** [ˋprɪzn̩] 名 監獄
▶ 延伸片語：**break prison** 越獄

怕輸

kiasu（名詞），（形容詞）

流行語解密！

kiasu 這個字源自新加坡，是閩南語「驚輸」的音譯。《牛津英語大辭典》(Oxford English Dictionary, OED) 於 2006 年將其收錄為英文字。根據 OED 的定義，kiasu 意為「（名詞）貪得無厭、自私自利的心態」/「（形容詞）害怕錯失機會的；貪婪的，貪得無厭的」。Urban Dictionary (UD) 則直截了當地將其直譯為 "afraid of losing out to other people, afraid to lose out"。由修杰楷、卜學亮等人主演的國片《做你愛做的事》，英文片名就叫做 Kiasu。事實上，OED 對「kiasu（怕輸）」的解釋並不是很貼切。「怕輸」應該是害怕吃虧，愛比較，輸人不輸陣，死愛面子之意，此乃華人社會的通病，不是嗎？

這樣用就對了！

1. I should have gone earlier, but now I am an hour late: the kiasu in me is growing.
   我原本應該提早去，但我現在已經遲到一小時了：現在我心裡越來越怕輸。

2. These parents are so kiasu! They send their children to cram schools before school starts.
   這些父母很怕輸在起跑點！學校都還沒開學，他們已經把他們小孩送去補習班了。

再學多一點！

★ **cram** [kræm] 動 把……塞進、狼吞虎嚥地吃東西

▶ 延伸片語：**cram into** 勉強塞入，填滿

記恨；記仇

hold a grudge (against someone) （動詞）

這片語中的 hold 亦可使用 bear 或 have 來代替。

這樣用就對了！

1. Deborah got the job I applied for, but I'm not one to bear a grudge.
黛柏拉得到了我申請的工作，但我不記仇。

2. Billy still has a grudge against Mary because she refused to go out with him years ago.
比利對瑪麗仍記恨在心，因為多年前她拒絕跟他交往。

3. She holds a grudge against the judge who sentenced her mother to death.
她對判她母親死刑的法官懷恨在心。

耍花樣

get cute （動詞）

流行語解密！

“get cute with someone” 意為「跟某人耍花樣」。這用法通常有負面的意味。另外這詞還有取笑的意思，例如：Don't get cute with Mary. Don't treat her as a crown. She helps us a lot.（別取笑瑪莉，不要把她當作小丑，她幫過我們大忙。）

這樣用就對了！

1. Don't get cute!
   別耍花樣！

2. Don't get cute with me, young man!
   別跟我耍花樣，年輕人！

Track 165

惡搞；搞笑；Kuso

spoof（動詞）；parody（動詞）

流行語解密！

spoof 和 parody 皆還可當名詞用。Parody 可以用在正式英文中，也可以當作一種諷刺的文學類別。惡搞或搞笑的人叫做 spoofer 或 parodist。spoofer 這個字在一般字典還查不到，僅網路字典 Urban Dictionary 有收錄。

這樣用就對了！

1. Some of his photos were spoofed by facebookers.
   他的一些照片遭到臉書用戶惡搞。

2. He parodied PSY's Gangnam Style.
   他把 PSY 的「江南 Style」搞笑一番。

3. This is a parody of PSY's Gangnam Style.
   這是 PSY「江南 Style」的 Kuso 版。

4. Johnny is such a parodist.
   強尼真是愛搞笑。

發酒瘋

get drunk and act crazy （動詞）

流行語解密！

get drunk 是喝醉的意思，act crazy 是說人行為舉止很瘋狂。這邊的 get 和 act 都當連綴動詞用，後面接形容詞。

這樣用就對了！

1. Martin usually gets drunk and acts crazy, throwing any object he sees.
   馬丁經常發酒瘋，看到東西就摔。

2. His father and mother were heavy drinkers and would often get drunk and act crazy, yelling at and even verbally abusing him.
   他的父母親過去都是酒鬼，經常發酒瘋，對他大吼大叫，甚至辱罵他。

Track 167

直覺；預感

gut feeling （名詞）

流行語解密！

gut 本身有「內臟」的意思，用在這裡是指內在的感覺，也就是直覺。我們亦可用 hunch（通常用單數）來表達相同的意思。

這樣用就對了！

1. My gut feeling is always right.
   我的直覺一向很準。

2. I have a hunch that I'm gonna fail my English exam.
   我有預感，我的英文考試會不及格。

看人（很）準

a good judge of character （名詞）

流行語解密！

我們可將 good 改為 excellent 來表示「看人很準」；若是看人不準，即「不會看人」，則用 a bad/poor judge of character 來表示。judge of character 是評斷人格特質的意思。

這樣用就對了！

1. I'm always an excellent judge of character.
   我一向看人很準。

2. My wife is a bad/poor judge of character.
   我太太不會看人。

瞎猜

a wild guess （名詞）；
have a wild guess （動詞）

have a wild guess 中的 have 可用 make 或 take 來代替。

這樣用就對了！

1. If you don't know the answer to the question, you can take a wild guess.
如果你們不知道這問題的答案，可以隨便瞎猜。

2. I just made a wild guess, but I really didn't know.
我只是瞎猜的，但我真的不知道。

路痴

someone has/ with no sense of direction （名詞）

流行語解密！

sense of direction 是方向感的意思，其中 sense 是「……感」，例如： sense of humor（幽默感）。沒有方向感除了 having no sense of direction 之外，亦可用 someone having/with poor sense of direction 來表示。

這樣用就對了！

1. People with no/poor sense of direction can easily get lost.
   路痴容易迷路。

2. I have no sense of direction at all.
   我是路痴。

3. My sense of direction is poor.
   我是路痴。

★ **sense** [sɛns] 名 感覺

★ **direction** [dəˋrɛkʃən] 名 方向

★ **humor** [ˋhjumɚ] 名 詼諧、幽默

★ **get lost** 片 迷路

Chapter 7

閨蜜聊八卦！

小確幸

a little happiness （名詞）

流行語解密！

小確幸指的是「小而確實的幸福」。台灣這句流行語來自日本小說家村上春樹的插畫散文集「尋找漩渦貓的方法」和「蘭格漢斯島的午後」。不過，英文早有 a little happiness 的說法。由於村上春樹也是美國文學翻譯家，說不定他是在翻譯美國文學作品或是在閱讀英文書籍時看到 a little happiness，而將之譯為「小確幸」？早在 1929 年，英國音樂喜劇作曲家 Vivian Ellis（男性；Vivian 是男女通用的英文名字） 就寫了一首傳唱至今、期間更被英國名歌手史汀（Sting） 翻唱且被 BBC 節目選為主題曲的民謠歌曲《Spread A Little Happiness》。美國唱作歌手愛咪艾倫（Aimee Allen） 2013 年發行的第二張專輯，名稱叫做《A Little Happiness》。此外，之前紅遍全台的電影主題曲《小幸運》，英文歌名也翻作 A Little Happiness。

必須注意的是，a little happiness 不能寫成 little happiness，因為 a little 表示少量，還有一點，是肯定的意思，而 little 表示少之又少幾乎沒有，是否定的意思。所以，little happiness 是表示「幾乎沒有的幸福」。土耳其一部 2013 年底發行、2014 年初在國際上映的電影，片名叫做《Little Happiness》，描述一對情侶不顧家人反對，私奔到一個小鎮過著恩愛的生活，但在兒子出生後，由於開銷增加，生活逐漸困頓，再加上女方賭博惡習復燃，兩人關係開始變調、惡化……，最後勞燕分飛，幸福蕩然。

這樣用就對了！

1. Money can't buy happiness for everyone, but it may be able to buy some people a little happiness.
   錢不能讓每個人都買到幸福，但也許可以讓一些人買到小確幸。
2. Capturing a little happiness is my way to live a happy life.
   抓住每天的小確幸是我開心生活的方法。

閨蜜

bestie

流行語解密！

最近很流行的詞彙「閨蜜」，意思是女生之間非常要好的朋友，也就是手帕交。在英文中 bestie 是「最好的朋友」的意思，跟中文一樣，通常是指女性之間的朋友。如果說男性間的朋友通常會用 buddy，形容好朋友的還有 confidante（知己）confidante 含有「吐露心事」的意味，也是指很好的朋友！另外還有 bff（best friend forever），confidante 跟 bff 都可以用在男性或是女性朋友間喔！

這樣用就對了！

1. Wendy and I were in the same kindergarten. She has been my bestie since then.
   溫蒂跟我念同所幼稚園，從那時候開始我們就一直是閨蜜。

2. My boyfriend is having an affair with my bestie.
   我男朋友跟我閨蜜有染。

★ **kindergarten** [ˋkɪndɚˏgɑrtn̩] 名 幼稚園

★ **have affair** 片 外遇

★ **confidant** [kɑnfɪˋdænt] 名 知己

★ **confidante** [kɑnfɪˋdænt] 名（女）知己，紅粉知己

▶ 相關詞：**confidential** [ˏkɑnfəˋdɛnʃəl] 形 祕密的

照騙

The picture certainly/surely (doesn't) flatter you.

流行語解密！

照片還可用 photo（複數 photos） 或 photograph 來表示。這句的關鍵字是 flatter，它除了「奉承；諂媚」的意思外，還意為「（相片、畫等） 比（真人） 好看」。視情況而定，句中的 you 可改為任何的人稱代名詞或名詞。當然了，我們亦可視需要加上 doesn't 表達「照片沒有本人好看」的意思。如果要用名詞，可以用 flattering photos。

這樣用就對了！

1. This picture surely doesn't flatter my wife.
   我太太這張照片沒有本人好看。
2. The photo flatters Amy.
   這張 Amy 很照騙。

八卦

gossip（名詞）、（動詞）

流行語解密！

gossip 可以是動詞或是名詞，如果當動詞可以在後面加上 about 表示「八卦關於某件事」。必須注意的是，並非所有「八卦」都可用 gossip 來表示。八卦媒體的英文叫做 tabloid，八卦

雜誌 tabloid magazines，而八卦網站叫做 tabloid websites。

這樣用就對了！

1 My wife enjoys gossiping with her friends.
我太太喜歡和她的朋友聊八卦。

2 She has a gossip with her neighbor every day.
她每天都和鄰居聊一下八卦。

走運

luck out （動詞）

流行語解密！

luck out為一片語動詞。out是「出來」的意思，跟台語的「出運」有異曲同工之妙。要注意的是在英式英文中 luck out 有完全相反的意思，是不幸的意思。

這樣用就對了！

1 You really lucked out avoiding the sentence.
你真走運，避免了刑罰。

2 The economy of this country lucked out for most of the decade.
這國家的經濟在這十年的大部分時間都鴻運當頭、福星高照。

一竿子打翻一船人

tar (somebody) with the same brush （動詞）

流行語解密！

tar 這個字當名詞時是「焦油、柏油」的意思，當動詞時意為「塗抹焦油」。這句話直譯是「用同一把刷子塗抹焦油」，引喻只要有一處沒塗好，就把其他的也當作不好，也就是一竿子打翻一條船的意思。

這樣用就對了！

1. Although she committed the crime, I'm not going to tar her friends with the same brush.
雖然她犯了刑，但我不會一竿子打翻一船人，也認為她的姊妹都犯罪。

2. I admit that some celebrities take drugs but it's not fair that we're all being tarred with the same brush.
我承認有些名人吸毒，但一竿子打翻一船人，認為我們都吸毒，那是不公平的。

★ **commit** [kə`mɪt] 動 委任、承諾

★ **crime** [kraɪm] 名 犯罪

★ **admit** [əd`mɪt] 動 承認

★ **celebrity** [sɪ`lɛbrətɪ] 名 名人

★ **drug** [drʌg] 名 藥物

▶ 延伸片語：**take drug** 吸毒

Track 177

一罪二罰；一事二罰；一頭牛剝兩次皮

double jeopardy（名詞）

流行語解密！

double jeopardy 字面的意思是「雙重危險」、「一行為重複處罰」或「重複追訴」，也就是「一罪二罰；一事二罰」，現在有時也用來表示「一頭牛剝兩次皮」的意思。但它真正的含意是在強調「一罪不二罰」、「一事不二罰」原則。根據美國憲法第五條修正案（the Fifth Amendment to the U.S. Constitution），「任何人均不得因同一罪名，使生命或肢體受到兩次危害」(...nor shall any person be subject for the same offence to be twice put in jeopardy of life or limb...)。Jeopardy 意為「危險，風險，危難」，是個不可數名詞。這裡為法律用語，指的是「（被告處於被判罪或受處罰的）危險境地」。相關的片語為：To be in jeopardy （處於危險中）；to put ／ place somebody ／ something in jeopardy（使某人／某事物處於危險之中）。

這樣用就對了！

1. The concept of double jeopardy is widely accepted.
   一罪不二罰 ／ 一事不二罰的觀念得到廣大的認同。

2. Double jeopardy is not fair.
   一事二罰 ／ 一頭牛剝兩次皮並不合理。

山寨版

knockoff（名詞）

流行語解密！

山寨版就是仿製品，尤指名牌仿製品，亦可用 knock-off products 來表示。

這樣用就對了！

1. Oh my gosh, is that Louis Vuitton?
   天哪！那是 LV 嗎？
   Nah, it's a knockoff, my mom got it for $5.
   不，那是山寨版，我媽媽用 5 塊錢買的

2. This Dior wallet is definitely a knockoff.
   這個迪奧錢包肯定是山寨版

3. Brooke knows the place to go for quality ╱ designer knockoffs.
   布魯克知道去哪裡買高級的仿製品╱山寨版的名牌服飾

Track 179

半開玩笑

half-joking/ half-jokingly（形容詞）,（副詞）

流行語解密！

副詞 half-jokingly 比形容詞 half-joking 來得常見許多。

這樣用就對了！

1. They seem to be only half-joking when they say he should run for president in 2020.
   當他們說他 2020 年應該競選總統時，他們似乎只是半開玩笑的

2. She suggested half-jokingly that we should sell our house and move to the suburbs.
   她半開玩笑地建議我們賣掉房子搬到郊區去

3. Half-jokingly, half-seriously, Hill told me that he would divorce his wife at the age of 70.
   半開玩笑、半認真地，希爾告訴我他七十歲時要跟他太太離婚。

冷笑話

dry humor（名詞）

流行語解密！

英文中的冷笑話跟中文有點不同，dry humor 是不動神色講出不涉及不雅卻又好笑的事情。如果要說某個人很會講冷笑話，可以說某人 have dry sense of humor。亦可說成或寫成 (a) dry sense of humor。

這樣用就對了！

1. His dry humor made us laugh our pants off.
   他的冷笑話使我們笑翻了。

2. Many people thought John had a dry sense of humor.
   許多人都認為約翰有講冷笑話的幽默感。

先有雞還是先有蛋？

Which came first, the chicken or the egg?

「先有雞還是先有蛋」是千古哲學思辨的問題。這句英文經常略作 the chicken and/or the egg?

這樣用就對了！

1. Do you know which came first, the chicken or the egg?
你知道先有雞還是先有蛋嗎？

2. What do you say when a kid asks you: "Which came first, the chicken or the egg?"
當小孩問你「先有雞還是先有蛋」時，你要怎麼說呢？

Track 182

全職媽媽

stay-at-home mom（名詞）

流行語解密！

stay-at-home 可當名詞和形容詞用，前者意為「深居簡出者，老是留在家裡的人，不愛出門的人，戀家的人」，後者意為「不愛出門的，戀家的」，這裡是用作形容詞。Stay-at-home mom 與 working mom 相對，後者意為「在職媽媽；上班族媽媽」，亦即有孩子的職業婦女或回家還要照顧小孩的職業婦女。

這樣用就對了！

1. My mom was a stay-at-home mom and she took care of and raised three kids.
   我母親過去是個全職媽媽，照顧和撫養三個小孩。

2. Most stay-at- home moms aren't rich.
   大多數全職媽媽並不富裕。

3. Working mothers feel that working is beneficial to motherhood and overall family life.
   上班族媽媽認為，工作有益於身為人母者及家庭整體生活。

Track 183

收拾心情

pick up the pieces（動詞）

流行語解密！

這句英文通常是用在受驚嚇、受災等情況之後要重振旗鼓。pick up the pieces 亦可表示「恢復正常；重振旗鼓」之意。

這樣用就對了！

1. After a while, Ted was able to pick up the pieces and carry on with his work.
   一會兒後，泰德就收拾心情繼續他的工作。

2. After quarrelling with his wife, Peter picked up the pieces at once and went to work.
   彼得和他太太爭吵後，馬上收拾心情去上班。

3. After Ruth's death, John found it hard to pick up the pieces and carry on with his life.
   露絲過世後，約翰發現他難以恢復正常，繼續過他的生活。

快閃店

pop-up store/shop（名詞）

快閃店是指廠商短期設立的商店或臨時櫃位，用來舉行限時、限量特賣活動。限時是快閃店的主要特色，短則幾天，長則幾個月又消失不見。雖然全球第一家快閃店早在 2003 年就已誕生於紐約，但快閃店在國內外都是一種新的營銷模式，將創意營銷模式與零售店面結合在一起。概念與此相似的快閃市集或市場（pop-up market）最近也越來越夯。

Pop-up 是個形容詞，意為「突然出現的；突然冒出來的」。不過，必須注意的是，大家熟知的「快閃族」，英文叫做 flash mob，與 pop-up 無關。快閃族現象也是在 2003 年開始席捲全球。另外，值得一提是，美國通常使用 pop-up store，而英國和澳洲大多使用 pop-up shop。事實上，現在 pop-up（用作名詞）單獨一個字有時就可表示快閃店的意思，尤其是在句意明確的上下文中，複數為 pop-ups。

這樣用就對了！

1. Several chic pop-up stores have popped up in Taipei in recent months.
   最近幾個月台北突然出現好幾家快閃潮店。

2. I am thinking about running a pop-up store because of the lower cost.
   我考慮開一家快閃店，因為這樣成本比較低。

炒作

publicity stunt （名詞）

流行語解密！

publicity 意為「宣傳」，而 stunt 為「特技」，兩者放在一起，a publicity stunt，就是「為了宣傳而使出的絕招」，也就是「炒作」。

這樣用就對了！

1. The haters regard the kindness of the politicians as a publicity stunt.
   酸民認為政治人物的善行不過是炒作而已。

2. The two movie stars' romance is a publicity stunt.
   這兩位電影明星的戀情是一項炒作。

★ **hater** [hetɚ] 名 酸民

★ **regard** [rɪˋgɑrd] 動 視為

▶ 相關詞：**regardless** [rɪˋgɑrdlɪs] 形 不在乎

★ **politician** [ˏpɑləˋtɪʃən] 名 政治家

▶ 相關詞：**politics** [ˋpɑləˏtɪks] 名 政治學／**political** [pəˋlɪtɪkḷ] 形 政治的

★ **romance** [roˋmæns] 名 羅曼史

扮白臉／黑臉

play good cop/bad cop （動詞）

流行語解密！

cop 是俚語中警察的意思，跟中文的「條子」意思雷同。一人或一些人扮白臉叫做 play good cop，而另一人或另一些人扮黑臉叫做 play bad cop。兩人或一群人有人扮白臉，有人扮黑臉，即未指明誰是白臉，誰是黑臉，則用 play good cop, bad cop 來表示。

這樣用就對了！

1. Mr. Smith often plays bad cop and Mrs. Smith plays good cop in educating and disciplining their children.
   在管教孩子方面，史密斯先生經常扮黑臉，而史密斯太太扮白臉。
2. GOP leaders play good cop/bad cop on raising taxes.
   美國共和黨領袖在增稅問題上，有人扮白臉，有人扮黑臉。

Track 187

泡（夜店）

hang out （動詞）

流行語解密！

hang out 意為「泡（在某地）；閒蕩，閒逛；廝混」。hang out（with + 人）（at/in + 地）意為「（和某人）泡（在某地）」。此外，hang out 也有「四處逛逛」」的意思，例如：I always hang out with my friends on the weekend.（我週末總是跟朋友四處晃晃）。

這樣用就對了！

1. He hangs out at the club The Princess; he's there most nights.
他都泡在「公主」夜店；大多數晚上他都在那裡。

2. Henry was always hanging out with his brother at the café.
亨利和他弟弟過去老是泡在咖啡店。

Track 188

喝酒壯膽

Dutch courage（名詞）

流行語解密！

這成語據說源於荷蘭（Dutch）軍隊作戰前喝酒的習慣，好讓自己有「酒後之勇」，更敢於衝鋒陷陣，但是 Dutch courage 也有「並非真的勇敢」，甚至有「膽小到需借酒壯膽」的意味。當時英國跟荷蘭海上爭霸賽競爭激烈，戰後英國極力抹黑荷蘭，所以現今英文中的 Dutch 大多是比較負面，或是跟酒相關的詞彙，例如：go Dutch（各付各的）、Dutch treat（各自買單的聚會）、Dutch headache（宿醉）、Dutch bargain（喝酒後的交易，指的是不牢靠的交易）。

這樣用就對了！

1. The mayor needed a bit of Dutch courage before he made an after-dinner speech.
市長需要先喝點酒壯壯膽，才敢發表餐後演說。

2. It was Dutch courage that made the criminal attack the policeman.
就是酒後之勇才使那個罪犯膽敢攻擊警察。

家族遺傳

run in the family （動詞）

流行語解密！

這是指特徵、特性、個性等為一家人或家裡許多人所共有。

這樣用就對了！

1. My grandparents and my father got the same illness and it runs in the family.
我祖父母跟我爸都有同樣的疾病，這是家族遺傳。

2. Both Teresa and her mother have snaggletooth. It runs in the family.
泰瑞莎和她母親都有暴牙。那是家族遺傳。

Track 190

一天一蘋果，醫生遠離我

An apple a day keeps the doctor away.

流行語解密！

雖然實際上蘋果並非萬靈丹，但蘋果對心血管確實有好處，也有助於調節血糖及控制食慾、預防癌症、保護肺部健康等等。

這樣用就對了！

1. I eat apples every day. An apple a day keeps the doctor away.
我每天都吃蘋果。一天一蘋果，醫生遠離我。

2 Grandma grew apples because she believed that an apple a day keeps the doctor away.
我奶奶種了很多蘋果，因為她相信一天一蘋果，醫生遠離我。

保存期限
shelf life（名詞）

流行語解密！

亦叫做 best-before date。保存期限在中國大陸叫做保質期。如果過期了，則會用 expired，expire 當動詞有「終止」、「期限已滿」、「過世」的意思。expire 的形容詞是 expiry，常說的有效期限英文是 expiry date。

這樣用就對了！

1 Milk normally has a shelf life of one week.
牛奶通常有一個禮拜的保存期限。

2 The best-before date of the food is six months.
這食物的最佳賞味期為六個月。

★ **shelf** [ʃɛlf] 名 架子

★ **normally** [ˋnɔrmlɪ] 副 正常地

Track 192

保固期限內

under warranty （片語）

流行語解密！

warranty 為產品的「保證書」、「保固（說明書）」。要說「（多久的）保固期」則是在時間後面加上 warranty period。

這樣用就對了！

1. Is the refrigerator still under warranty?
這台冰箱還在保固期限內嗎？

2. This smartphone has a one-year warranty period.
這支智慧型手機有一年的保固期。

Track 193

拿得出去的／拿不出去的

presentable / unpresentable （形容詞）

流行語解密！

presentable 亦可表示「像樣的」意思，而 unpresentable 則亦可表示「不像樣的；見不得人的」意思。這兩個字互為反義詞。可以用來形容東西或是人。

這樣用就對了！

1. All his oil paintings are presentable artwork.
他的所有油畫都是拿得出去的藝術作品。

❷ My wife never gives me a presentable birthday gift.
我太太從未送我一樣像樣的生日禮物。

❸ A little bird told me that Leo's relatives are all unpresentable.
有人告訴我，李歐的親戚沒有一個像樣的。

甄選；海選

open audition （名詞）

流行語解密！

上下文句意夠明確的話，僅用 audition 亦可。在公開甄選中，過關叫做 to make the cut、被選中叫做 to be ／ get selected，而被刷下來、被淘汰叫做 to be ／ get eliminated。

這樣用就對了！

❶ An estimated 4,500 "Star Wars" fans attended open auditions for next film, which is due out in 2015. Only three of them made the cut to advance to the next round, and the others all got eliminated.
估計約有 4,500 名《星際大戰》的粉絲參加將在 2015 年上映的下一部影片的甄選。只有三人被選中，進入下一輪甄選。其餘的人全部被刷了下來。

❷ "America's Got Talent" will kick off open auditions for Season 9 on October 26. The audition cities include Miami, Atlanta, and Los Angeles.
《美國達人秀》將於 10 月 26 日開始進行第 9 季的海選。舉辦甄選的城市包括邁阿密、亞特蘭大和洛杉磯。

盡地主之誼
do the honors （動詞）

盡地主之誼意思是主人或是當地人招待來訪的親友，包括供應餐飲、招待用餐、招呼和介紹客人等。

這樣用就對了！

1. Jack, I need to go into the kitchen for a moment, so why don't you do the honors and get Susan a drink?
傑克，我需要進去廚房一下，所以你何不盡一下地主之誼，給蘇珊弄點喝的呢？

2. You do the honors and pour out the tea while I bring in the cakes.
你盡一下地主之誼，給客人倒茶，我去把糕餅拿來。

3. John was asked to do the honors during his best friend's wedding.
在他最要好朋友的婚禮上，約翰被請求招待賓客。

Track
196

搞錯方向
off (the) beam （形容詞）

流行語
解密！

雖然這片語的意思就是「錯誤的；不準確的」(mistake, incorrect, wrong)，它原指飛機或船隻偏離了無線電信號指引的航向，而 beam 本身有「電波」、「對準」的意思。相反詞為 on (the) beam（搞對方向）。

這樣用就對了！

❶ Sue's assignment was entirely off beam.
蘇的工作完全搞錯方向。

❷ What the minister said about the new policy was way off the beam.
這位部長對新政策所發表的言論完全搞錯方向。

再學多一點！

★ **assignment** [əˋsaɪnmənt] 名 作業

★ **minister** [ˋmɪnɪstɚ] 名 神職者、部長

Track 197

土生土長；生於斯長於斯

born and bred（形容詞）

流行語解密！

這個形容詞可以放在 be 動詞之後或者表示某地區或某地方之人的名詞之後。born 是（被）生下來而 bred 是（被）餵養。

這樣用就對了！

❶ He was born and bred in the Pescadores but now lives in Kaohsiung.
他是土生土長的澎湖人，但現在住在高雄。

❷ Jack's a Londoner born and bred.
傑克是土生土長的倫敦人。

Chapter 8

耍廢豬隊友別雷我！

我會罩你
I'll watch your back.

流行語解密！

這裡的 watch 意為「小心，留心，注意」，但必須注意的是，watch one's back 有兩個截然不同的意思：若要表示「罩」的意思，則主詞和 one's 必須是不同的人；如果主詞和 one's 為同一人，那麼這片語就意為「提防（周遭的人）」。

這樣用就對了！

1. I'll watch your back at this end. You can count on me.
   在我這頭，我會罩你。你可以信賴我。

2. John told me he would watch my back in the math exam.
   約翰對我說，數學考試他會罩我。

3. Life's too short to have to watch your back all the time.
   人生苦短，不必一直提防別人。

★ **count on** 片 依賴

▶ 相關詞：**count** [kaʊnt] 動 數

★ **Life's too short.** 俚 人生苦短

Track 199

不怕神一樣的敵人，只怕豬一樣的隊友
With friends like that, who needs enemies?

流行語解密！

這是一句從網路上流行起來的說法，也可以簡稱為「豬隊友」，可能是打遊戲組隊或是做分組報告時，結果自己的隊友一直扯後腿，後來也很常用在其他需要與他人一起努力的活動上面。With friends like that, who needs enemies? 則是英文固有的用法，直譯是「有這樣的朋友，誰還需要敵人？」跟中文的「不怕神一樣的敵人，只怕豬一樣的隊友」有異曲同工之妙。

這樣用就對了！

1. With friends like that, who needs enemies? We lost the game because my friend killed me.
   不怕神一樣的敵人，只怕豬一樣的隊友，我們輸了這場遊戲，因為我的隊友殺了我。

2. When we were about to make a presentation, my teammate accidentally deleted our group report. With friends like that, who needs enemies?
   當我們要上台報告的時候，我的組員不小心把我們小組報告給刪掉了。不怕神一樣的敵人，只怕豬一樣的隊友。

再學多一點！

★ **presentation** [ˌprɛznˋteʃən] 名 呈現；上台報告

很雷

slack（形容詞）/slacker（名詞）

流行語解密！

這詞從線上遊戲中紅到日常生活中，很雷是形容人沒有幫自己人，甚至是害到隊友。之後衍生出雷包，雷神索爾這些名詞，如果是被隊友陷害則是說被雷，如果是吃到不好的餐廳則是踩雷。在英文中，會用 slack 說人很雷，可能他是有能力的卻故意用很鬆散的態度做事，如果用 slacker 則是稱呼很雷的人，也就是雷包。

這樣用就對了！

1. He is so slack that he puts off our proposal again and again.
他很雷，一次又一次地遲交我們的提案。

2. You are such a slacker that I don't want to play the game with you.
你那麼雷，我不想要再跟你同隊了。

Track 201

耍廢

veg out（動詞）

流行語解密！

耍廢也是近年來流行的語彙，說整天無所事事，本來英文中有 idle（形容詞，無所事事），但是近年來 veg out 成了最流行的詞彙，成日看電視看電腦耍廢。另外整天坐在沙發上看電視的人也被稱作 couch potato（沙發馬鈴薯）。

這樣用就對了！

1. The typhoon gave us an excuse to veg out whole day.
   颱風給了我們理由可以整天耍廢。

2. Should I get married with my girlfriend who does nothing but veg out?
   我該跟我女朋友結婚嗎？她成日無所事事只會耍廢。

Track 202

正經事；不是開玩笑的事

no laughing matter （名詞）

流行語解密！

這慣用語通常與 be 動詞連用，放在 be 動詞之後。

這樣用就對了！

1. Be serious! This is no laughing matter.
   別開玩笑了！ 這是正經事。

2. Think twice before you adopt that Chihuahua. Taking care of a pet is no laughing matter.
   你養那隻吉娃娃之前要想好哦。養寵物可不是開玩笑的。

再學多一點！

★ **think twice** 片 三思

打開天窗說亮話

talk turkey （動詞）

流行語解密！

這用法主要用於美國。源自美國拓荒時期，有一位白人跟印第安人一起打獵，打到了一隻烏鴉跟一隻火雞，白人想要火雞又不好意思，所以就跟印第安人說：「如果我拿火雞的話你就拿烏鴉，不然就你拿烏鴉我拿火雞吧！」結果印第安人一眼識破白人的詭計，要白人別拐彎抹角了，說：「跟我直說『把火雞給我』吧！（Talk turkey to me!）」後來這句話衍生成「打開天窗說亮話」的意思。

這樣用就對了！

1. Richard wanted to talk turkey, but Janet just wanted to joke around.
理查想要談正經事，但珍妮只想鬧著玩，開開玩笑。

2. I took my business friends out for dinner and then talked turkey with them.
我請生意上的朋友去外面吃飯，然後打開天窗說亮話，跟他們談正事。

★ **turkey** [ˋtɝkɪ] 名 火雞

★ **joke around** 片 開玩笑

★ **business** [ˋbɪznɪs] 名 商業、買賣

▶ 延伸片語：**business trip** 商務旅行、出差

Track 204

（做某事）看時間和場合；（做某事）分清楚時間和場合

There's a time and a place (for something).（片語）

流行語解密！

There's a time and a place 後面通常接 for 再接名詞。

這樣用就對了！

1. How could Felicia wear a dress like that to a wedding? Honestly, there's a time and a place.
費麗莎怎麼可以穿著那種服裝去參加婚禮呢？真是的，做事情要看時間和場合。

2. Don't show me your new bras in the street. There's a time and a place for that sort of thing.
不要在大馬路上給我看你新買的內衣。做那種事要分清楚時間和場合。

再學多一點！

★ **wedding** [ˋwɛdɪŋ] 名 婚禮、結婚
▶ 延伸片語：**go to the wedding** 參加婚禮

★ **honestly** [ˋɑnɪstlɪ] 形 誠實的、耿直的
▶ 延伸片語：**honestly = to be honest** 老實說

議價空間；降價空間

wiggle room（名詞）

流行語解密！

在其他方面，wiggle room（不可數名詞）表示「（外交、談判、解釋或表達等的）彈性空間；迴旋餘地」。

這樣用就對了！

1. A: Is there any wiggle room on that price?
   A：那個價格還有議價／降價空間嗎？
   B: I'm afraid that's as low as I can go (on that price).
   B：我恐怕那是我所能給的最低價了。

2. We need to leave ourselves some wiggle room.
   我們必須留給自己一些彈性空間。

Track 206

獅子大開口；搶錢

highway robbery; daylight robbery（名詞）

流行語解密！

highway robbery 為美式英語，而 daylight robbery 為英式英語。

這樣用就對了！

1. The amount of money that the company is charging for its services is sheer highway robbery.
那家公司索取的服務費金額完全是獅子大開口。

2. Two hundred NT dollars for a black tea? That's just highway robbery!
紅茶一杯 200 塊台幣？簡直就是搶錢！

3. It was just daylight robbery for the price of the concert tickets!
音樂會門票的價格簡直是搶錢！

置入性行銷

product placement（名詞）

亦可用 embedded marketing 來表示，但較少見，其中 embed 是「嵌入」的意思。

這樣用就對了！

1. Product placement subtly advertises products in TV programs.
置入性行銷巧妙地在電視節目為商品做廣告。

2. Product placement in films and international programs (such as US drama series) has been allowed on UK television for many years.
英國電視允許影片和國際節目－如美國戲劇影集－的置入性行銷已經好多年。

潛規則

unspoken rule（名詞）

流行語解密！

跟潛規則類似的詞彙是不成文規矩（unwritten rule），例如：It is an unwritten rule never to disturb my work in my family.（在我家，不可以打擾我工作，是一項不成文規定）

這樣用就對了！

1. A lot of people suspected that there were some unspoken rules in the contest.
   許多人懷疑該比賽有一些潛規則。

2. The competition was not fair. It was following some unspoken rules evidently.
   這項競賽不公平，因為它遵循一些潛規則。

Track 209

朝九晚五

nine-to-five（形容詞）

流行語解密！

朝九晚五是說（工作）從早上九點到晚上五點，亦寫成 9-to-5。朝九晚五的上班族叫做 nine-to-fiver (9-to-5er)。

這樣用就對了！

1. That's a nine-to-five job.
那是一份朝九晚五的工作。

2. My father is only a regular nine-to-fiver.
我父親只是一個平凡的朝九晚五上班族。

★ **regular** [ˋrɛgjələ] 形 規律的

菜鳥

newbie（名詞）rookie（名詞）

流行語解密！

newbie 原指電腦或網路的新手。如果是校園或是職場的菜鳥，可以用 rookie，其中 rook 是一種叫做白嘴鴉的鳥類，而加上 -ie 意思是小的，所以 rookie 是小鳥，也就是菜鳥的意思。

這樣用就對了！

1. He doesn't know how to drive yet; he's a newbie.
他還不知道怎麼開車；他是個菜鳥。

2. He is a rookie. Teach him what to do.
他是個菜鳥。告訴他要做什麼。

入錯行

in the wrong line of business （片語）

流行語解密！

line of business／work 意為「行業」，例如：What line of business is your sister in exactly?（你姊姊究竟從事什麼行業？）

這樣用就對了！

1. It appears that I'm in the wrong line of business after seeing what they charge per hour of labor.
在看了他們每個工時的收費之後，我似乎入錯行了。

2. I think Martha is in the wrong line of business. With her expertise, she should consider a job in law.
我認為瑪莎入錯行了。以她的專業知識，她應該考慮從事法律工作。

★ **appear** [əˋpɪr] 動 出現，顯得
 ▶ 延伸片語：**it appears to me that...** 據我看來
 ▶ 延伸片語：**as is appears** 似乎

★ **charge** [tʃɑrdʒ] 動 索價、命令／ 名 費用、職責
 ▶ 延伸片語：**in charge (of)** 看管、負責管理

★ **labor** [ˋlebɚ] 名 勞力／ 動 勞動
 ▶ 延伸片語：**Labor conquers all things.**
 勞動會戰勝一切。

★ **expertise** [ɛksˋpɚtɪz] 名 專家鑑定

老鼠會

pyramid scheme（名詞）

流行語解密！

又稱「金字塔式騙局」。老鼠會在大多數國家都是非法的。至於合法的「多層次傳銷」，英文叫做 multi-level marketing，經常縮寫為 MLM。

這樣用就對了！

1. That's a pyramid scheme! Don't fall for it!
   那是老鼠會！別受騙上當！

2. Quite a few people think that multi-level marketing (MLM) is, in reality, the legalized version of a pyramid scheme.
   相當多的人認為，多層次傳銷實際上是合法版的老鼠會。

★ **pyramid** [ˋpɪrəmɪd] 名 金字塔
★ **scheme** [skim] 名 計畫
★ **fall for** 片 受……騙，愛上……，遭受不光彩的事情
★ **reality** [rɪˋælətɪ] 名 現實
★ **legalize** [ˋligḷaɪz] 動 合法化
★ **version** [ˋvɜʒən] 名 版本

詐騙集團

scam gang （名詞）

流行語解密！

scam 這個字可當名詞和動詞用，意為「詐騙（錢財）」。電話詐騙集團叫做 phone scam gang，而詐騙電話為 scam phone call。

這樣用就對了！

1. Scam gangs have a bag of tricks.
   詐騙集團有各種詐騙手法。

2. The police cracked down a phone scam gang.
   警方破獲了一個電話詐騙集團。

3. I get scam phone calls two or three times a month.
   我每個月接到兩三次詐騙電話。

Track 214

陷阱；圈套；隱情；詭詐

catch （名詞）

流行語解密！

在口語中，這個字往往用於 What's the catch? 此一問句中，而 What's the catch? 已成為表示「其中有何陷阱／圈套／隱情／

詭詐？」的固定用語，用來詢問一件容易或美好的事情其中是否有陷阱、圈套、隱情或詭詐。

這樣用就對了！

1. There is a catch to that last question.
最後那道問題有陷阱 ／ 最後那道問題是陷阱題。

2. This looks like a good deal. What's the catch?
這看起來像是一項不錯的交易。其中有詐嗎？

3. This price sounds too good to be true. What's the catch?
這價格聽起來好得不像是真的。有什麼陷阱 ／ 隱情嗎？

Track 215

內神通外鬼

an inside job（名詞）

流行語解密！

an inside job 亦有「監守自盜」之意。

這樣用就對了！

1. The bank robbery was an inside job.
這起銀行搶案是內神通外鬼。

2. There is a growing number of Americans who believe 9/11 was an inside job.
越來越多的美國人認為，911 恐怖攻擊事件是內神通外鬼。

走後門；打通關節；幕後牽線

pull a few strings（動詞）；pull some strings（動詞）

這成語的基本型態為 to pull strings，但慣用的說法是 to pull a few strings 或 to pull some strings。

這樣用就對了！

1. Cindy's father pulled a few strings for her to get a job in that state-owned enterprise.
   辛蒂的父親走後門，為她在那家國營企業謀得一職。

2. I know more than a few politicians, so if you have any trouble, I can pull some strings for you.
   我認識不少政界人士，所以如果你有任何麻煩的事情，我可以幫你打通關節。

挖角

poach （動詞）

流行語解密！

poach 還有「偷獵，盜獵」、「用水煮（蛋等）；用文火燉（食物）」等意思，都相當常見，如 poached eggs（水煮蛋）。

這樣用就對了！

1. John's manager was poached by a competitor.
約翰的經理已被該公司的競爭對手挖角了。

2. Japanese baseball teams seem to be poaching all our best players.
日本棒球隊似乎要把我們最好的球員都挖走。

師父引進門，修行在個人

You can lead a horse to water, but you can't make it/him drink.

流行語解密！

這句亦可說成 You can take a horse to water, but you can't make him drink.，字面意思為「你可以牽馬到水邊，但你不能強迫牠喝水」。

這樣用就對了！

1. Mason always complains about not having enough money. I showed him an ad I saw for a part-time job. He said it was a good idea, but he never called the phone number. I guess you can lead a horse to water, but you can't make it drink.
梅森老是抱怨錢不夠用。我給他看一個兼職廣告，他說不錯，可是從不打電話去問。我認為師父引進門，修行在個人。

2. She is the best teacher in the school. But your son doesn't make any improvement. I think you can lead a horse to water, but you can't make it drink.
她已經是全校最好的老師了，但你兒子都沒有進步，我覺得師父領進門，修行在個人。

前途無量

go places （動詞）

流行語解密！

go places 意思是未來很有可能會成功、勝出。要注意 place 須用複數。

這樣用就對了！

1. The first time we watched Jeremy Lin play basketball on TV, we knew he would go places.
我們第一次在電視上看林書豪打籃球時，就知道他前途無量。

2. Melissa is such a gifted musician that I always believe she's going places.
馬莉莎是位極有天賦的音樂家，我一直相信她前途無量。

★ **promising** [ˋprɑmɪsɪŋ] 形 有前途的

★ **gifted** [ˋgɪftɪd] 形 有天賦的、有才能的

▶ 延伸片語：**gifted child** 天才兒童

▶ 延伸片語：**be gifted with** 賦予

▶ 相關詞：**gift** [gɪft] 名 禮物、天賦

▶ 延伸片語：**have a gift for...** 對……有天賦

★ **musician** [mjuˋzɪʃən] 名 音樂家

窮忙族

the working poor（名詞）

流行語解密！

窮忙族是指一些人很努力工作，但是收入卻無力跳脫貧困甚至無法負擔生活所需之開銷，又稱作薪貧族，若是青年族群則稱作青貧族。窮忙的英文則是 working poverty。

這樣用就對了！

1. Single parents with young children can easily become members of the working poor.
子女年幼的單親媽媽和爸爸很容易變成窮忙族。

2. I am one of the new working poor, and so are many of my friends.
我是新的窮忙族，我的許多朋友也是。

Track 221

忙死了

drowning（形容詞）

流行語解密！

英文應該還有其他用語可以表達「忙死了；忙極了」的意思，如 hands are full，但 drowning 本意是「將要溺斃」，所以最傳神、最道地。

這樣用就對了！

1. I'm literally drowning in five translation cases right now.
我現在手邊有五個翻譯案件要完成，簡直忙死了。

2. My husband's really drowning and he's been working overtime almost every day for more than three months.
我先生真是忙死了，三個多月來，他幾乎每天加班。

3. Benjamin has his hands full with three app development projects right now.
班傑明現在手邊有三個應用程式開發案要完成，他忙極了。

和時間賽跑

race against time（動詞），（名詞）

流行語解密！

race 可以是名詞或動詞。

這樣用就對了！

1. As animators, we were always in a race against time to beat the deadline.
身為動畫家，我們總是和時間賽跑，趕在最後期限之前完成。

2. We had to race against time to finish before the deadline.
我們必須和時間賽跑，趕在最後期限之前完成。

3. You don't need to race against time. Take your time!
你不必趕時間。慢慢來！

月光族

someone living from paycheck to paycheck（名詞）

流行語解密！

對於每月把收入花光光的人，現在我們稱之為「月光族」。Paycheck 是付薪水的支票，所以這是說人一拿到薪水就花掉了。

這樣用就對了！

1. Eugene has been living from paycheck to paycheck for ages.
   長期以來尤金一直是個月光族。

2. I don't want to be a person who lives from paycheck to paycheck.
   我不想當月光族。

Track 224

哭窮

poor-mouth/poormouth（動詞）；poor mouth（名詞）

流行語解密！

poor-mouth 的時態變化為 poor-mouths, poor-mouthed, poor-mouthing。

這樣用就對了！

1. Tom is always poor-mouthing that he doesn't have any money, but he just bought a brand-new BMW.
湯姆老是哭窮，說他沒有錢，但他剛買了一部全新的 BMW。

2. He did nothing but poormouthed all day long.
他整天除了哭窮，什麼也沒做。

3. Blanche: I couldn't pay the bill.
布蘭奇：我付不起賬單。
Joseph: Stop crying poor mouth, you lie!
約瑟夫：別哭窮了，妳說謊！

Track 225

無殼蝸牛

Generation Rent（名詞）

流行語解密！

無殼蝸牛（有時也稱無殼族或無殼蝸牛族）指的是無力購買房屋（尤其是在房價急速飆漲的區域購屋），包括使用房屋貸款（mortgage or mortgage loan）購屋，而必須租屋生活的人。

這樣用就對了！

1. Four in five of those classified as "generation rent" have no prospect of owning a home in the next five years.
在那些被歸類為「無殼蝸牛」的人士當中，每五人就有四人在未來五年間沒有買房的可能性。

2. The number of people in "Generation Rent" has increased dramatically in recent years.
近年來無殼蝸牛族的人數急遽增加。

光說不練

be all mouth and trousers; be all mouth and no trousers; be all mouth （動詞）

流行語解密！

這三個成語當中，以 be all mouth 的語氣最弱；它們都在表達「只會坐而言，不會起而行」的意思。

這樣用就對了！

1. His trouble was that he was all mouth and trousers.
   他的毛病就是光說不練。

2. We did not vote for him because he was known to be all mouth and no trousers.
   我們沒有投票給他，因為大家都知道他只會坐而言，不會起而行。

低調一點

keep a low profile （動詞）

流行語解密！

keep a low profile 就是叫人行事保持低調，以免招惹麻煩，其中 low profile 意為「低調」，相反詞為 high profile，即「高調」。keep 可以用 maintain 來替換，但 keep a low profile 比 maintain a low profile 常見許多；然而，maintain a high profile（保持高調）卻比 keep a high profile 來得常見。

這樣用就對了！

1. Mason's been keeping a low profile at work ever since his argument with Tony.
自從跟東尼爭吵後，梅森上班時一直保持低調。

2. The outsiders are warned to keep a low profile while visiting this area.
外地人被告誡在參訪這地區時要保持低調。

★ **profile** [ˋprofaɪl] 名 人物簡介

★ **maintain** [menˋten] 動 維持

▶ 延伸片語：**maintain peace** 維護和平

★ **argument** [ˋɑrgjəmənt] 名 爭論、議論

▶ 相關詞：**argue** [ˋɑrgjʊ] 動 議論

▶ 相關詞：**dispute** [dɪˋspjut] 動 爭論

找碴；過不去

pick on (somebody)（動詞）

流行語解密！

pick on (somebody) 這個片語動詞的意思就是「找（某人）的碴；跟（某人）過不去」，其中受詞 somebody 只能放在介系詞 on 的後面，不可說成或寫成 to pick somebody on。pick 的形容詞 picky 意思是很龜毛。

這樣用就對了！

1. Professor Anderson often picks on us.
   安德森教授經常找我們的碴。

2. Why does John always pick on me?
   約翰為什麼老跟我過不去呢？

盯得很緊；盯得死死地

breathe down someone's neck（動詞）

流行語解密！

父母盯著子女、老師盯著學生、老闆或上司盯著員工，都可用這成語來表示，即緊緊盯住某人。

這樣用就對了！

1. It's awful having to work with a boss who's breathing down your neck all the time.
非得在老闆在旁邊一直盯著的情況下工作，真叫人受不了。

2. I can't work with you breathing down my neck the whole time. Go away! Stop breathing down my neck.
你老是在一旁盯著我，我沒辦法幹活。走開！別再緊盯著我。

Track 230

抓茫

the choking game （名詞）

流行語解密！

這是歐美中學校園流行的一種窒息遊戲，經由網路影片傳到國內。抓茫（閩南語發音）是在有人進行激烈運動，氣喘吁吁時，或有人先蹲下起立時，再由其他人摀胸、勒脖，用各種方式妨礙對方呼吸，使對方因缺氧而昏倒。據醫學專家表示，短暫窒息會讓人有失神、解離的感覺，過程中也會跟吸毒者一樣產生快感、幻覺及暈眩感。然而，國內已陸續傳出抓茫受傷事件，國外更有死亡案例，因此是一種危險性相當高的遊戲，千萬不要嘗試。The choking game 在國外亦被稱為 space monkey（太空猴）、the pass out game（昏倒遊戲）或 the fainting game（昏倒遊戲）。

這樣用就對了！

1. Wanna go play the choking game?
想玩抓茫窒息遊戲嗎？

2. The choking game is very dangerous. Don't try this at home, school, or anywhere.
抓茫非常危險。別在家裡、學校或任何地方嘗試。

Chapter 9

我就是不爽你咬我啊！

你爸媽現在在後面，他們很火

PAW(parents are watching)

流行語解密！

這句話直譯是「你的爸媽正在看你」，在英文中通常是形容因為父母在所以小孩比較收斂，用在中文就是「你的爸媽現在在後面，他們很火」，用來說人別做壞事。

這樣用就對了！

1. You are staying up late to watch films again? PAW!
   你又在熬夜看影片了喔？你爸媽在後面，他們很火。

2. You are going to Hong Kong for the girl? PAW!
   你為了那女孩要去一趟香港？你爸媽在後面，他們很火。

Track 232

臉上三條線

speechless（形容詞）

「臉上三條線」是源自卡通裡面用來表示無言、傻眼時會在卡通人物臉上劃三條直線，後來「臉上三條線」就用來表示「(啞口)無言；傻眼」。

這樣用就對了！

1. Mrs. Huang was speechless when she saw several topless photos of her daughter online.
黃太太在網路看到她女兒的上空照時當場臉上三條線。

2. I was really speechless about his rude behavior at the restaurant last night.
對於他昨晚在餐廳的粗魯行為，我真是臉上三條線。

Track 233

翻白眼

roll one's eyes (at someone) （動詞）

流行語解密！

這通常表示不悅、不耐煩或不相信。

這樣用就對了！

1. Don't roll your eyes at me!
不要對我翻白眼！

2. My wife rolled her eyes (at me) when I asked her not to dress that way.
當我要求我太太不要那樣穿時，她對我翻白眼。

★ **roll** [rol] 動 轉動

倒胃口

turn-off（名詞）

流行語解密！

倒胃口字面上的意思是吃得很飽，以至於看到其它食物都反感，後來衍生是對東西反感的意思。這句英文除了 turn-off，亦可用動詞型態 to turn off 來表示。不過要注意的是，相反詞 turn someone on 常常具有性暗示的意思。

這樣用就對了！

1. That movie was a real turn-off so I left early.
   那部電影真是讓我倒胃口，所以我就提前離開了。

2. The music totally turned me off so I asked my son to turn the TV off.
   那音樂讓我倒盡胃口，所以我就叫我兒子把電視關掉。

3. My girl friend's new pajamas really turn me on.
   我女朋友的新睡衣真的讓我很有「性」致。

Track 235

別慌；別著急

Don't have a cow!

流行語解密！

亦可用 chill out 來表示，意思與 calm down 相同，chill 有「冷」的意思，所以 chill 是要人冷靜一下。不過，chill out 還意為「放鬆一下」(relax)。

這樣用就對了！

1. Don't have a cow! I'll give you a hand with your homework.
別慌！你的家庭作業我會助你一臂之力。

2. Chill out, man!
老兄，別著急！

Track 236

放心
rest assured （動詞）

流行語解密！

常用於祈使句，其句型為 Rest assured that ／ You can rest assured that ＋名詞子句，其中 assured 為形容詞，意為「有把握的；自信的；肯定的」。

這樣用就對了！

1. You can rest assured that your daughter will be happy here.
你可以放心，你女兒在這裡會快樂的。

2. You can rest assured that we will do our best.
請放心，我們會盡最大努力。

3. Rest assured that those guys won't bother you again.
你放心好了，那些傢伙不會再打擾你。

再學多一點！

★ **assure** [əˋʃʊr] 動 向……保證、使確信

▶ 延伸片語：**assure sb. that** 使某人確信

想開了；想通了

be over it（片語）

流行語解密！

英文還有一句含意相近的口語 to get over it，同樣表示對痛苦或難過的事情會「想通的」、「撐下去」、「熬過去」或忘了那些不愉快的事情。

這樣用就對了！

1. I suffered for days after Hilary broke up with me, but I'm over it now.
希拉蕊跟我分手後，我難過了好幾天，但現在我想開了。

2. A:Sorry about standing you up last night.
抱歉，昨晚放你鴿子。
B:Whatever, I'm over it.
無所謂，我想開了。

3. Amy was so heartbroken when her parents split up, but she said she would get over it.
艾美父母離異時，她傷心欲絕，但她說她會熬過去的。

★ **suffer** [ˋsʌfɚ] 動 痛苦

★ **split** [splɪt] 名 裂口／ 動 劈開、分化
▶ 動詞變化：**split, split, split**
▶ 延伸片語：**split up** 分異

覺得賭爛；嘔氣；賭氣；生悶氣

snit（名詞）

流行語解密！

通常以片語 in a snit 的型態出現。snit 是名詞，就是生悶氣、嘔氣的意思。

這樣用就對了！

1. Todd's been in a snit all morning.
   陶德整個早上都在嘔氣。

2. Yvonne's been in a snit ever since her boyfriend grabbed Olivia's ass.
   伊芳自她男友抓了奧莉薇的屁屁後一直生著悶氣。

倒楣

a tough break（名詞）；have a tough break（動詞）；tough luck（名詞）

流行語解密！

break 在此當名詞用，意為「良機；好運」。而 tough 則是不幸的意思，所以 tough break 就是不好的運氣，也就是倒楣的意思。

這樣用就對了！

1. You got in an accident! Tough break!
   你發生意外！你真倒楣！

2. Jack had a lot of tough breaks when he was a kid, but he's doing okay now.
   傑克小時候衰事連連，但現在運氣不錯。

3. When a beggar approached us, Mary murmured "tough luck" and then gave him a few coins.
   當有個乞丐靠近我們時，瑪麗輕聲地說「真倒楣」，然後給了他幾個銅板。

★ **accident** [ˋæksədənt] 名 事故

★ **beggar** [ˋbɛgɚ] 名 乞丐

★ **approach** [əˋprotʃ] 動 接近

★ **murmur** [ˋmɝmɚ] 動 輕聲細語

擺臭臉

mean mug （動詞）

流行語解密！

這兩個字合起來當動詞用，其中 mean 意為「意圖；打算」，而 mug 為俚語，意為「扮鬼臉；做怪相」。mean mug 後面往往接人當受詞，即 to mean mug someone，意為「對某人擺臭臉」。

這樣用就對了！

1. Why are you mean mugging?
   你為何擺著一副臭臉呢？

2. The chick in the party was mean mugging me all night.
   派對上那個妞整晚都對我擺著臭臉。

Chapter 10 就是要互動！

你少臭美了
You're full of yourself.

流行語解密！

be full of oneself 意為「自吹自擂；自以為是」，也就是「臭美」的意思。不過，當我們說「你太臭美了」時，其中隱含的是「你少臭美了；你別臭美了」的意思。反身代名詞 oneself 須視主詞人稱而做適當的變化。

這樣用就對了！

1. Maria is very unpopular because she's too full of herself.
   瑪麗亞很不得人緣，因為她太自以為是了／她太臭美了。
2. A: I think I'm a metrosexual and I can attract a lot of women.
   我認為我是型男，能吸引許多女人。
   B: You're full of yourself.
   你少臭美了。

Track 242

拍馬屁
brown nose （動詞）; suck up （動詞）; brown nosing/brown-nosing （名詞）

流行語解密！

brown nose 亦寫成 brown-nose，可作及物或不及物動詞。suck up 為不及物動詞，若要接被拍馬屁的人，其後還要使用 to 再接人，即 suck up to someone。

這樣用就對了！

1. John is always brown nosing his superior.
= John is always sucking up to his superior.
約翰老是拍他上司的馬屁。

2. Hey Jack, stop sucking up to Harry!
嗨，傑克，別再拍哈利的馬屁了！

3. I don't like Jason because he brown-noses our boss very often.
我不喜歡傑森，因為他常常拍老闆的馬屁。

教你幾招
teach you a thing or two （動詞）

流行語解密！

這句話的本意是「很擅長某件事情」，也就是中文的「可以教你幾招」，teach you a thing or two 後面往往接介系詞 about 來表示在某方面或就某事教你幾招。這句話也可以說 tell you a thing or two。

這樣用就對了！

1. Never done wrestling before? I can teach you a thing or two.
沒試過摔角嗎？我可以教你幾招。

2. I can teach you a thing or two about Internet dating.
關於網路交友，我可以教你幾招。

放我一馬

let me off the hook （動詞）

流行語解密！

get/let someone off the hook 意為「放某人一馬」；be/get off the hook 意為「脫身」，即擺脫責任、麻煩或困境。

這樣用就對了！

1. I don't believe his boss let him off the hook again.
   我不信他老闆又放他一馬了。

2. Thanks for letting me off the hook. I didn't want to meet him.
   感謝放我一馬。我不想看到他。

3. Larry's just happy to be let off the hook on that harassment charge.
   賴瑞很高興能從那項騷擾指控脫身。

4. Amy tried to get off the hook by blaming Wendy.
   艾美想藉由責備溫蒂來擺脫責任。

★ **hook** [hʊk] 名 鉤、鉤子／ 動 鉤、用鉤子鉤住

▶ 延伸片語：**hook on to** 鉤住，追隨

★ **harassment** [həˋræsmənt] 名 騷擾

★ **blame** [blæm] 名 責備

★ **charge** [tʃɑrdʒ] 名 控告，索賠

唬爛你的／騙你的

psych（感嘆詞）

流行語解密！

這個字有時被拼成 sike, syke 或 sych 等。psych 在非正式英文中可以當作動詞，意思是「使人驚嚇、緊張」，如果放在生活對話中，講了一句話讓人激動，然後說 psych（我只是嚇嚇你的），就是「耍你的」啦！

這樣用就對了！

1. Mary, you look so beautiful today. Psych!
   瑪麗，妳今天看起來好美。耍妳的！

2. Don't worry baby, I love you ... I will never leave you. Psych!
   別擔心，寶貝，我愛妳……我絕不會離開妳。騙妳的！

3. John: Sure, I'll lend you 1,000 dollars.
   約翰：沒問題，我會借你 1 千元。
   Peter: Really?
   彼得：真的嗎？
   John: Psych!
   約翰：騙你的！

晾在一邊

leave someone hanging （動詞）

流行語解密！

這裡要表達的是讓他人等你的答案等得很久，也就是「把某人晾在一邊」。這慣用語源自兩個人見面，其中一人舉手要擊掌（high five），但另一人卻沒有舉手，使得前者舉起的手晾在半空中。

這樣用就對了！

1. You were supposed to be one of my best friends, but you really left me hanging when you talked with that hottie.
你原本是我最好的朋友之一，但當你在跟那位辣妹交談時，卻把我晾在一邊。

2. Don't leave me hanging—I'm counting on you.
別把我晾在一邊—我都靠你了。

Track
247

順著（某人的意思）

humor (someone) （動詞）

流行語解密！

humor 這個字平常看到的是它的名詞「幽默」，但是它也可以當動詞，意為「遷就」。

這樣用就對了！

1. It's out of the question for me to humor you. Cut it out!
我不可能順著你的意思。別鬧了！

2. It's usually unwise to humor a child.
遷就小孩子通常是不明智的。

Track 248

打槍／潑冷水
throw cold water on something （動詞）

流行語解密！

打槍的本意是「拒絕」、「退貨」，但是現在衍生的用法有「不認同」、「讓人打退堂鼓」，在英文中的 throw cold water on something 意思是「讓人打消念頭」，中文可以翻作「打槍」或是「潑冷水」。其中throw亦可用pour來代替，亦即「潑冷水」也可用 pour cold water on something 來表示。

這樣用就對了！

1. The plan seemed reasonable enough, but the CEO quickly threw cold water on it.
這計畫似乎滿好的，但執行長馬上就對其潑了冷水。

2. My father poured cold water on my plans by saying I couldn't study abroad.
我父親對我的計畫潑了冷水，他說我不能出國唸書。

3. I thought the girl was fond of me, but she poured cold water on me by saying she has a boyfriend.
我覺得那女生喜歡我，但是她打槍我了，她說她有男朋友了。

會吵的小孩有糖吃

The squeaky wheel gets the grease.

流行語解密！

這句話中，squeaky 是「吱吱叫的」，wheel 是「輪子」，而 grease 則是「（潤滑）油」，這句話直譯是「會吱吱叫的輪子才會上油」，也就是中文的「會吵的孩子有糖吃」。亦可用 The squeaky wheel gets the oil. 來表示，但比較少見。

這樣用就對了！

1. No matter what computer they give her, Mary generally insists on a better one and she gets it. The squeaky wheel gets the grease.
   不管他們給她什麼電腦，瑪麗通常會堅持要一部更好的，而且都會得到，因為會吵的小孩有糖吃。

2. Nina begged for months to her parents for a new car and she somehow got it. The squeaky wheel gets the grease, I guess.
   妮娜要她父母買新車已吵了好幾個月，不知用了什麼方法，她如願以償了。我想這就是會吵的小孩有糖吃。

Track 250

下逐客令

show the door （動詞）

流行語解密！

這句話字面的意思是「告訴某人門在哪裡」，也就是下逐客令的意思。通常以 show someone the door 的型態出現，意為「對某人或向某人下逐客令」。

這樣用就對了！

1. I was shown the door when I hit him.
在我打了他之後就被下了逐客令。

2. I criticized her boyfriend. Then, she showed me the door.
我批評她的男朋友，然後我就被下逐客令了。

3. Dickson was rude to my family and I simply showed him the door.
狄克森對我家人粗魯無禮，所以我就對他下了逐客令。

再學多一點！

★ **criticize** [ˋkrɪtəˏsaɪz] 動 批評、批判

▶ 延伸片語：**criticize sb. for doing sth.** 批評某人做了某事

★ **rude** [rud] 形 魯莽的

Track 251

撂狠話

talk tough （動詞）

流行語解密！

tough 在此用作副詞。例句中的 act tough 意為「來硬的，硬起來，採取強硬的作為」，用法與 talk tough 同。

這樣用就對了！

1. Professor Lee has talked tough to all of us.
李教授已對我們所有人都撂下狠話。

2. I can talk tough and scare that guy, but I can't really act tough.
我可以撂狠話嚇嚇那個傢伙，但我不能真的來硬的。

鬧翻

falling out（名詞）

亦寫成 falling-out，為可數名詞，複數為 fallings-out 或 falling-outs。

這樣用就對了！

1. Tim isn't gonna attend my birthday party tomorrow because we had a falling out last week.
提姆不會參加我明天的生日派對，因為我們上週鬧翻了。

2. Stanley had a falling-out with his parents yesterday.
史丹利昨天跟他父母鬧翻了。

打群架

donnybrook（名詞）

亦可用 free-for-all 來表示。Donnybrook 是愛爾蘭首都都柏林（Dublin）的一處郊區，當地以喜歡吵架而聞名。也可以寫作 donnybrook。

這樣用就對了！

1. Adam got seriously hurt in a donnybrook last night.
亞當昨晚打群架受到重傷。

② The supporters from both sides began shouting insults at each other and then got into a real free-for-all.
雙方的支持者開始互罵，然後大打出手。

互不相欠

even-steven;
even-stevens（形容詞）,（副詞）

流行語解密！

even-steven 和 even-stevens 分別為美式和英式英語口語，除了「互不相欠」外，它們還意為「機會相等；均等的 / 均等地（每人所擁有或提供的數量、金額相等）」。even-steven 和 even-stevens 通常有連字號，但 steven 和 stevens 都是小寫，從不大寫。

這樣用就對了！

① Give me 100 dollars and we're even-steven.
給我 100 元，我們就互不相欠了。

② They split an inheritance even-steven.
他們平分了遺產。

★ **inheritance** [ɪnˋhɛrətəns] 名 遺產

Chapter 11

團購什麼搶手貨我都要跟！

丁字褲／小丁

thong（名詞）

女性的性感丁字褲也被現代人暱稱為小丁。thong 這個字本來是皮革的意思，現在多當作丁字褲解釋，可能指女性的性感內褲或是相撲或是一些原住民的傳統服飾，在美國也有「人字拖（鞋）；夾腳拖（鞋）」的意思；人字拖或夾腳拖在英國叫做 flip-flop。

這樣用就對了！

1. My boyfriend likes to remove my thong during sex.
   我男友喜歡在嘿咻時扯掉我的丁字褲。

2. What a thong!
   好誘人的丁字褲啊！

Track 256

高腰褲

high-rise jeans（名詞）

流行語解密！

現在流行高腰褲以增長腿的比例，高腰褲的英文是 high-rise jeans, high-slung trousers, high-cut jeans，另外，低腰褲是 hipsters, hip-huggers, low-riders 和 low-slung trousers 等數種不同的講法，其中以 high/low-rise jeans 最常見。

這樣用就對了！

❶ Nowadays, many youngsters like to wear high-rise jeans.
時下年輕人喜歡穿著高腰褲。

❷ Ginny was wearing a pair of low-rise jeans and showing her thong at the party last night.
吉妮昨晚在派對上穿著低腰褲並露出丁字褲。

Track 257

免治馬桶
Washlet/ washlet (toilet seats)（名詞）

流行語解密！

Washlet 原為免治馬桶生產廠商日本東陶公司（TOTO）的註冊商標，但與 Band-Aid（OK 繃）、Chap stick（護唇膏）、Hi-Liter（螢光筆）、Kleenex（面紙）、Popsicle（冰棒）、Post-it（便利貼）、Q-Tip（棉花棒）、Saran wrap（保鮮膜）和 Scotch tape（膠帶）等字一樣，現已「商標品名普通名詞化」，泛指所有的免治馬桶。

這樣用就對了！

❶ More and more people try to use Washlet.
越來越多人嘗試使用免治馬桶。

❷ Some houses in our community have installed washlets (or washlet toilet seats).
本社區的一些房子已經安裝免治馬桶。

Track 258

博愛座

priority seat/seating（名詞）

流行語解密！

priority seat 為可數名詞，而 priority seating 為不可數名詞。在若干英語系國家，除了博愛座外，有些大眾運輸工具上還設有 courtesy seating (禮貌座)。博愛座是給身障人士坐的，而禮貌座是給年長者、孕婦、抱著嬰兒或帶著幼童的成人坐的。

這樣用就對了！

1. You can see priority seats on most public transportation in Taiwan.
你可以在台灣的大多數大眾交通工具上看到博愛座。

2. Priority seating is for the use of passengers with a disability.
博愛座是給身障乘客使用的。

Track 259

行車記錄器

dashboard camera（名詞）

流行語解密！

簡稱 dash cam 或 dashcam。

這樣用就對了！

1. A dashboard camera is an excellent tool to record traffic accidents.
行車記錄器是記錄交通事故的利器。

② There are many kinds of dashcams in the market.
目前市面上有很多種行車記錄器。

★ **excellent** [ˋɛksḷənt] 形 最好的

Track 260

伴手禮

souvenir（名詞）

流行語解密！

伴手禮就是紀念品，台語又叫做「擔路」，香港叫「手信」。

這樣用就對了！

① Those Chinese tourists spent the whole morning buying souvenirs.
那些中國觀光客整個上午都在採購伴手禮。

② Jack bought a few pineapple cakes as souvenirs of his holiday in Taiwan.
傑克買了一些鳳梨酥作為他在台灣度假的伴手禮。

★ **tourist** [ˋtʊrɪst] 名 觀光客

★ **pineapple** [ˋpaɪn͵æpḷ] 名 鳳梨

刷爆（信用卡）

max out (somebody's credit card)（動詞）

流行語解密！

這是主動態，但我們也可用被動態，即「信用卡被刷爆了」，甚至可以說「某物太貴，會使信用卡刷爆」。

這樣用就對了！

1. Did you ever max out your credit card?
   你曾經刷爆信用卡嗎？

2. Your card is maxed out.
   你的卡刷爆了。

3. This watch will max out my credit card.
   這支錶會使我的信用卡刷爆。

Track 262

刮刮樂

scratch-off (lottery ticket)（名詞）

流行語解密！

scratch 是刮的意思，而 scratch-off lottery ticket 就是刮刮樂囉！例如：Tom won $50,000 on a $3 scratch-off.（湯姆買了一張三美元的刮刮樂，刮中了五萬美元。）注意 on 放在彩券或刮刮樂的前面，表示該張彩券或刮刮樂（上面的號碼或金額組合）中了或刮中了多少金額。

這樣用就對了！

1. Tina is too addicted to scratch-offs. She buys one every day.
   堤娜太沉迷於刮刮樂了，她每天都會買一張。

2. A scratch-off lottery ticket recovered from the trash won a Taitung couple NT$ 10 million.
   一張從垃圾中找回來的刮刮樂，讓台東一對夫妻刮中了台幣一千萬。

Track 263

中頭彩

hit the jackpot （動詞）

流行語解密！

jackpot 是累積獎金，hit the jackpot 除了中頭彩，也衍生出「獲得良機」、「十分幸運」的意思。彩券叫做 lottery 或 lottery ticket；樂透則是 lotto (ticket)。

這樣用就對了！

1. Hitting the jackpot is everyone's dream.
   中頭彩是每個人的夢想。

2. Hitting the jackpot will make you (a) billionaire.
   中頭彩將使你成為億萬富豪。

★ **billionaire** [ˏbɪljənˋɛr] 名 億萬富翁

王牌；殺手鐧；法寶；秘密武器

an ace in the hole（名詞）

流行語解密！

亦可用 an ace up one's sleeve 來表達相同的意思。這句話是來自撲克牌中，ace 是最強的一張牌，如果把它藏在孔洞或是衣袖裡面，等到重要時刻才打出來，就是王牌了。

這樣用就對了！

1. The police have several aces in the hole to deal a devastating blow to the drug smugglers.
警方現有數個能給予毒梟毀滅性打擊的殺手鐧。

2. The basketball team has an ace up their sleeve with their new player.
那支籃球隊的新球員是該隊的王牌。

★ **sleeve** [sliv] 名 袖子

★ **devastating** [ˋdɛvəs͵tetɪŋ] 形 具有毀滅性的

▶ 相關詞：**devastate** [ˋdɛvəs͵tet] 動 毀滅

★ **smuggler** [ˋsmʌglɚ] 名 走私者

▶ 相關詞：**smuggle** [ˋsmʌgl] 動 走私

老千

cardsharp, card shark（名詞）

流行語解密！

card shark 亦指牌藝熟練、精湛的人，因此未必全然帶貶義。但 cardsharp（亦寫成 card sharp）則一定指打牌詐賭的人。cardsharping（名詞）意為「出老千」。

這樣用就對了！

1. Don't play Steve, he's a cardsharp.
   別跟史蒂夫玩牌，他是老千。

2. You always lose money by playing with a card shark.
   跟老千打牌一定輸錢。

搶手貨

something selling like hotcakes（名詞）

流行語解密！

sell like hotcakes 的意思是「暢銷，熱賣」，所以 something sells like hotcakes 就是「熱銷商品，搶手貨」。不過，sell like hotcakes 亦可寫成 go like hotcakes，只是後者比較少見。事實上，英文還有一個成語可表達與 sell like hotcakes 完全相同的意思，那就是 fly off the shelf。

這樣用就對了！

1. Dragon Year commemorative coin sets sold/went like hotcakes.
   龍年紀念套幣是搶手貨。

2. Foreign wines have flown off Taiwan's supermarket shelves.
   外國葡萄酒在台灣超市一直很暢銷。

3. A new kind of over-the-counter (OTC) medicine for flu is expected to fly off the chemists' shelves.
   一種新的流感成藥料將在藥房熱賣。

限量版

limited edition（名詞）

流行語解密！

這一用語往往後接名詞來表示「限量版的……」，例如：limited

edition cellphone（限量版的手機）。limit 是限定的意思，limited 則是形容詞；意為「限定的」。

這樣用就對了！

1. This store only sells women's limited edition clothing.
   這家商店只販賣女性限量版衣服。

2. You can buy the latest limited edition brochure from the website.
   你可從該網站購買最新的限量版小冊子。

Track 268

復刻版

replica edition（名詞）

流行語解密！

「復刻」這一詞是來自日本，一開始指稱重製絕版的書籍，後來廣泛使用在唱片等其他產業。而 replica edition 這一用語往往後接名詞，例如：replica edition book（復刻版書籍）。replica 是複製品的意思，在展覽中如果看到文字說明是 replica 則代表這不是真跡。

這樣用就對了！

1. The newspaper has launched its replica edition App.
   這家報紙已推出該報的復刻版應用程式。

2. These types of replica edition sneakers sell well.
   這種復刻版運動鞋賣得很好。

穿越劇

time travel TV series （名詞）

流行語解密！

time travel 是時空旅行的意思，在西方一直有 time travel 的故事，例如 1895 年 H. G. Well 的科幻小說 The Time Machine《時光機器》，或是 2003 年出版 2009 年翻拍成電影的 Time Traveler's Wife《時空旅人之妻》。用在電視影集上變成 time travel TV series 則是穿越劇的意思，其中 series 以及 means 和 species 是英文中少數幾個以 s 做結尾的單複數同形字。

這樣用就對了！

1. Time travel TV series have become very popular in recent years.
近年來，穿越劇變得非常流行。

2. The company has a new time travel TV series in the works which has a cast of several rising stars and child stars.
那家公司正在籌備一部新的穿越劇，卡司陣容有數位新秀和童星。

Track 270

公仔

action figure（名詞）

流行語解密！

“action figure”這個術語是由全球第二大玩具製造商，美國的孩之寶公司 (Hasbro) 於 1964 年首先創造出來的。早期最流行的是超人等造型的公仔。通常由塑膠製成，可以活動手腳。現在公仔的尺寸有很多種，可能小到花生米大，也可能大到跟人一樣大。

這樣用就對了！

1. Norman has collected many different kinds of action figures.
   諾曼已收藏許多不同種類的公仔。

2. There are several little action figures on my desk.
   我的書桌上有幾個小公仔。

杯緣子

fuchico（名詞）

流行語解密！

杯緣子為近幾年來很夯的小公仔，是一個身穿藍衣、綁著雙馬尾的辦公女性，俏皮的坐在杯緣的公仔，療癒了很多上班族的心情，受歡迎程度使得高人氣的扭蛋機（gachapon）往往扭出來就是杯緣子。杯緣子來自日文，fuchi 是日文邊緣、杯緣的意思，co 是日文的「……子」所以被翻成杯緣子。

這樣用就對了！

1. There is a fuchico on Linda's cup.
   琳達的杯子上有個杯緣子。

2. I play gachapon to collect the latest version of fuchico.
   我扭扭蛋是為了要蒐集最新版的杯緣子。

買一送一

twofer; bogof（名詞）

流行語解密！

twofer 亦可當形容詞用。bogof 為 buy one get one free 的頭字語，可以當作名詞。

這樣用就對了！

1 The deal is a twofer. Buy one get one free.
這項交易是買一送一。

2 This is a twofer dress.
這件女裝買一送一。

3 There are always some great twofer on at the outlet.
暢貨中心總是有很棒的買一送一優惠。

Track 273

團購
group buying（名詞）

流行語解密！

也稱為 group purchasing。團購是近年來網路購物盛行後廣為流行的一種行銷模式，意思是一群人一起合買某樣商品，因而獲得優惠折扣。也有人覺得團購是一種促銷的花招或噱頭（gimmick）。

這樣用就對了！

1 Nowadays more and more people like group purchasing online.
現今越來越多人喜歡網路團購。

2 Miss Tsai is a group buying maniac.
蔡小姐是個團購狂。

再學多一點！

★ **maniac** [ˋmenɪ͵æk] 名 狂熱者

Chapter 12

鮮肉肥宅妹子
恐龍妹的特質！

人魚線

V-line abs （名詞）

亦可叫做 V abs，其中 abs 就是「腹肌」(abdominals)。

這樣用就對了！

1. Nowadays a lot of men work on their V-line abs.
現今許多男性都在練人魚線。

2. Obtaining V-line abs isn't something that's going to happen overnight.
人魚線不是一天練成的。

六塊肌；腹肌

abs; six-pack （名詞）

six-pack 原指「六瓶裝；六罐裝」，如 a six-pack of beer（一箱六瓶裝的啤酒）。後來也用來指稱六塊肌。

這樣用就對了！

1. That hunk has chiseled abs.
那個猛男擁有如鑿刻般的六塊肌。

2. This is the fastest way to get a six-pack.
這是練成六塊肌最快的方法。

啤酒肚

beer belly（名詞）

流行語解密！

亦叫做 keg（原意為「啤酒桶」），但 beer belly 較常用許多。

這樣用就對了！

1. My father has got a beer belly.
   我父親有啤酒肚。

2. Sit-ups really help people lose their beer bellies.
   仰臥起坐真的有助於消除啤酒肚。

再學多一點！

beer-bellied 形 有啤酒肚的

pot-bellied 形 大肚子的

bulging waistline [委婉] 腰際線突出

▶ 相關詞：**bulging** [ˋbʌldʒɪŋ] 形 鼓起的

▶ 相關詞：**waistline** [ˋwestˏlaɪn] 名 腰圍

central obesity [醫] 中圍肥胖

★ **obesity** [oˋbisətɪ] 名 肥胖

游泳圈（腰部贅肉）

spare tire (tyre); love handles（名詞）

流行語解密！

這專門指腰部或腰間贅肉。至於身體上的任何贅肉，都可用 extra meat on the bones 來表示。

這樣用就對了！

1. No one likes their spare tire.
   沒有人喜歡自己的「游泳圈」。

2. If you want to get rid of your love handles, you should do more exercise.
   如果你想消除身上的游泳圈，你應該多運動。

★ **handle** [ˋhændḷ] 名 把手

★ **spare tire** 名 備胎

▶ 相關詞：**tire** [taɪr] 名 輪胎

▶ 相關詞：**spare** [spɛr] 形 剩餘的／動 節省、騰出

▶ 延伸片語：**spare a thought for...** 為……著想
get rid of 片 擺脫
exercise [ˋɛksɚˏsaɪz] 名 運動

Track 278

蝴蝶袖

bingo wings（名詞）

流行語解密！

美國上了年紀的胖女人贏賓果時往往會振臂歡呼，使得手臂下方鬆弛、低垂的肌肉有如翅膀般地拍動著，因而得名。

這樣用就對了！

1. I hate my bingo wings.
   我討厭自己的蝴蝶袖。

2. Tina wants to get liposuction to get rid of her hideous bingo wings.
   蒂娜想要抽脂來去除難看的蝴蝶袖。

3. Hannah has the largest bingo wings I've ever seen.
   漢娜的蝴蝶袖是我所見過最大的。

★ **liposuction** [ˋlɪpo͵sʌkʃən] 名 抽脂

▶ 相關詞：**tummy tuck** 縮腹手術
breast enlargement 隆胸；隆乳
brow lift 額頭拉皮手術
lip augmentation 豐唇手術

★ **hideous** [ˋhɪdɪəs] 形 令人贈恨的

遠看像朵花，近看像苦瓜；遠看像朵花，近看像她媽

fifty-footer（名詞）

流行語解密！

fifty-footer 意思是要在五十步之外看才好看，就是近看就不好看的人喔！這意思亦可用形容詞片語 “good from far, but far from good” 來表示。

這樣用就對了！

1. The chick that was walking in my direction was damn hot, and then I put on my glasses and realized she was a fifty-footer. Damn glasses!
   那個朝我這方向走來的妞真是他媽的辣，於是我就戴起了眼鏡，這才發現她是遠看像朵花，近看像苦瓜。該死的眼鏡！

2. That girl next door is totally a fifty-footer!
   鄰家那個女孩十足是個遠看像朵花，近看像苦瓜的醜八妹！

3. Mary was good from far, but far from good!
   瑪麗遠看像朵花，近看像她媽！

★ **chick** [tʃɪk] 名 小雞／俚 少女

★ **damn** [dæm] 形 該死的／副 完全的／感嘆詞 討厭／動 指責、輕蔑

▶ 延伸片語：**damn with faint praise** 明褒實貶

醜不拉嘰

plug-ugly（形容詞）

流行語解密！

當然了，亦可用 very ugly 或 extremely unattractive 等來表示相同或近似的意思，但它們都沒有這個字來得傳神。Plug-ugly 主要是個美式英語單詞，plug 和 ugly 之間有連字號。這個字還可當名詞用，意為「流氓；惡棍；幫派份子」，複數為 plug-uglies。

這樣用就對了！

1. That old lady has a plug-ugly old bulldog.
   那位老太太養了一隻醜不拉嘰的老鬥牛犬。

2. Paul may be plug-ugly, but he's such a gentle and loving boy.
   保羅雖然很醜，但他是個非常溫和可愛的男孩。

★ **plug** [plʌg] 名 塞子／俚 瑕疵品、滯銷貨

★ **extremely** [ɪk`strimlɪ] 形 非常的

★ **unattractive** [ə`træktɪv] 形 吸引人的、動人的

▶ 延伸片語：**attractive to sb.** 對某人具有吸引力

★ **bulldog** [`bʊl͵dɔg] 名 惡犬

★ **gentle** [`dʒɛntl̩] 形 和善的

還過得去

pass in a crowd（動詞）

流行語解密！

可指人或事物的還過得去、還可以、馬馬虎虎。這個詞往往用來形容人的外貌還過得去。

這樣用就對了！

1. Of course my wife is no beauty but I suppose she'll pass in a crowd.
   我太太當然不是美女，但我想她的容貌還過得去。

2. Jack's not exactly handsome, but he would pass in a crowd.
   傑克不是十分俊俏，但還過得去。

3. That proposal may pass in a crowd.
   那個提案可能還可以。

Track 282

俏麗短髮

pixie cut（名詞）

流行語解密！

pixie 這個字可當名詞和形容詞用，前者意為「小精靈；小妖精」，後者意為「調皮搗蛋的」。女子頭髮長度到脖子中間的髮型叫做 bob（波波頭；齊短髮）。

這樣用就對了！

❶ Hairstylist: What kind of haircut would you like this time?
髮型設計師：妳這次想剪什麼髮型呢？
Linda: I want a pixie cut.
琳達：我要剪俏麗短髮。

❷ Many Hollywood celebrities have a pixie cut hairstyle.
好萊塢許多名流都留了一頭俏麗短髮。

Track 283

股溝妹

coin slut（名詞）

流行語解密！

股溝的英文有十數個之多，甚至更多，其中 intergluteal cleft, gluteal cleft, natal cleft 為醫學或正式用語。carpenter's crack, plumber's crack 和 builder's bum 顯然跟職業有關，因為木工、水電工和建築工人在工作時經常會低身彎腰而露出股溝；不過，plumber's crack 是加拿大、澳洲和美式英語，而 builder's bum 是英式英語。至於由 ass, arse, bum, butt 等所構成的用語則皆為俚語。有趣的是，credit card swiper（刷卡機）和 coin slot（投幣孔）也被用來表示股溝。由於 slut （原意為「賤貨；蕩婦」）與 slot 的發音類似，因此美式俚語就以 coin slut 來指「股溝妹」；不過，根據 Urban Dictionary，此一俚語中的 slut 並無這項負面、貶抑的意思，只是指時常露股溝的女子。

這樣用就對了！

❶ Invest in a belt, you coin slut.
買一條腰帶吧，妳這個股溝妹。

❷ Mona is such a coin slut because she often wears low-rise jeans.
夢娜真是個股溝妹，因為她經常穿著低腰褲。

賣萌

cutesy（形容詞）

流行語解密！

cutesy 還有裝可愛、肉麻的意思，cutesy 的比較級為 cutesier，最高級為 cutesiest。

這樣用就對了！

1. Cindy's dress and hair are so cutesy.
   辛蒂的穿著和頭髮都很會裝可愛。

2. Earl sent me one of those awful greeting cards with a cutesy puppy on it.
   厄爾把那些驚人的賀卡寄了一張給我，卡片上有一隻賣萌的小狗。

3. That birthday card is too cutesy.
   那張生日賀卡太肉麻了。

Track 285

療癒系

comfort（名詞）

流行語解密！

療癒系是指漫畫、小説、電視節目等文藝創作、食物或商品，給人一種唯美、舒適、愉悦、欣喜等方面的心理感受，進而達到心情或情緒上的撫慰作用。現代人工作忙碌、生活緊張、心靈空虛，壓力沉重，療癒系可發揮一定程度的撫慰作用和紓壓

效果。與日本的視覺系偶像明星或商品一樣，療癒系的商機越來越大。注意：Comfort 的後面係直接接名詞來表示具有療癒系作用的人事物，但可別跟 woman 連用，因為 comfort woman/women 是「慰安婦」。

這樣用就對了！

1. I gotta get some comfort food.
   我必須弄些療癒系食物來吃。

2. Some people think that The Simpsons is comfort TV.
   一些人認為《辛普森家庭》是個療癒系電視節目。

裝可憐

give someone puppy (or puppy-dog) eyes（動詞）

這英文的意思就是睜大眼睛，像小狗一樣裝可憐。

這樣用就對了！

1. My little daughter gives me her puppy eyes every time she wants to play with my iPhone!
   我的小女兒每次要玩我的 iPhone 時都會裝得楚楚可憐！

2. Gary always gives his mother his puppy-dog eyes when he asks her for some money.
   當蓋瑞向他母親要錢時，他總是裝可憐。

Track 287

愛哭鬼

crybaby（名詞）

流行語解密！

亦寫成 cry baby 或 cry-baby。

這樣用就對了！

1. Peter is a crybaby because he cries too much.
彼得是個愛哭鬼，因為他太愛哭了。

2. You're such a crybaby.
你真是個愛哭鬼。

Track 288

擺架子；裝腔作勢；裝模作樣

airs and graces（名詞）

流行語解密！

英文中還有幾個成語可以表達相同的意思，它們是 give oneself airs, put on airs 及 put on the dog。

這樣用就對了！

1. Patricia has lost many friends because of her airs and graces.
派翠西亞喜歡擺架子，結果失去了許多朋友。

② Despite her fame, the actress has no airs and graces.
這位女星雖然名氣大，但從不擺架子。

臭屁

cocky（形容詞）

流行語解密！

cocky 這個字來自 cock 雄鳥，總是很威猛的樣子，cocky 亦可用 stuck-up 來表達相同的意思。

這樣用就對了！

① Peter is so cocky, and nobody really likes him.
彼得很臭屁，沒有人真的喜歡他。

② Tom is self-complacent and cocky.
湯姆自我感覺良好而且臭屁。

③ A new colleague of mine is rather stuck-up.
我的一位新同事相當臭屁。

再學多一點！

★ **stick** [stʌk] 動 釘住，黏住

▶ 動詞變化：**stick-stuck-stuck**

▶ 延伸片語：**stuck-with** 無法擺脫

★ **complacent** [kəmˋplesn̩t] 形 自我滿足

▶ 相關詞：**self-complacent** 形 自大的
colleague [ˋkalig] 名 同事

自我感覺良好

self-complacent（形容詞）；self-complacency（名詞）

流行語解密！

complacent 是個貶義詞，意為「自滿的，自鳴得意的，沾沾自喜的」。它的名詞為 complacence 或 complacency。「自我感覺良好」現在普遍被視為一個人的「自戀」。自戀的英文是 narcissism，形容詞 narcissistic，源於希臘神話中的 Narcissus，因為中了愛神邱比特的箭，因而愛上自己在水中的倒影，最終溺水而亡。

這樣用就對了！

1. The state of the economy is worsening, so there is no reason for the government to be self-complacent.
   經濟狀況日趨惡化，政府沒有理由自我感覺良好。

2. The president's self-complacency has brought about a lot of negative criticism and emotional attacks.
   總統的自我感覺良好招致許多負面批評及情緒性抨擊。

Track 291

控制狂

control freak（名詞）

流行語解密！

control 是控制的意思，像是遙控器的英文就是 remote control（remote 遙遠的），而 freak 可當形容詞形容人很奇怪，

它當名詞用時意為「怪人」，例如：Louis's kind of a freak.（路易斯這個人有點怪）。

這樣用就對了！

1. Ruby's boss is such a control freak. He has to review and approve everything she does!
露比的老闆是個控制狂。她所做的每件事都要他看過和批准！

2. Bullies are a special type of control freak.
霸凌者是一種特殊類型的控制狂。

Track 292

有潔癖的人
neat freak（名詞）

流行語解密！

freak 是「怪誕」、「不正常」的意思，neat 則是「乾淨、整潔」的意思，所以 neat freak 就是有潔癖的人，亦可用 clean freak 來表示。「有潔癖的人」在中國大陸叫做「整潔控」。潔癖的英文為 mysophobia，是由希臘字 mysos（不乾淨）＋ phobia（恐懼症）所組成的，以後看到 -phobia 結尾的字就有「恐懼……」的意思，像是：gynophobia（厭女症）。

這樣用就對了！

1. Holly is such a clean/neat freak! She cleans her house thoroughly every day and also irons all her kids' clothes.
荷莉真的是個有潔癖的人！她每天會把房子整個打掃一遍，也會把她小孩的衣服全部燙一遍。

2. Most people are not clean/neat freaks.
大多數人都沒有潔癖。

Chapter 13

這，就是人生！

Track 293

人生本來就是這麼回事
That's the way the cookie crumbles.

流行語解密！

這成語字面的意思是「餅乾掉到地上就會碎掉」，用來比喻人生本來就是這麼回事，因此當希望落空或遭遇不幸、不好或不如意的事情時可別太在意，也不要氣餒或惱怒。美國還有 That's the way the ball bounces. 的說法。

這樣用就對了！

1. I can't believe they chose Peter for the job but not me. Ah well, that's the way the cookie crumbles.
我不敢相信，他們竟然挑選彼得來擔任這項工作而不是我。啊，算了，人生就是這麼回事。

2. You'll just have to accept this result. That's the way the ball bounces.
你只能接受這項結果。人生本來就是這麼回事。

★ **crumble** [ˋkrʌmbl̩] 動 粉碎
★ **bounce** [baʊns] 名 彈、跳／ 動 彈回
▶ 延伸片語：**bounce back** 捲土重來，很快恢復
★ **accept** [əkˋsɛpt] 動 接受
★ **result** [rɪˋzʌlt] 動 結果

回不去了

There can be no going back.

流行語解密！

這句話是在電視劇《犀利人妻》中，外遇的丈夫乞求妻子回到身邊，妻子含淚說：「可是瑞凡，我回不去了。」因而大紅，後來這句不僅限用於男女或婚姻關係，舉凡無法回頭或沒有退路的情況，甚至是無法用原先的角度看待事情都可用它來表示。

這樣用就對了！

❶ My husband has told me his affair with that woman is at an end although they remain friends. And he has told me he still loves me, but I say there can be no going back after what has happened.
我先生對我說，他跟那女人的戀情已經結束，不過他們還是朋友。他也對我說，他仍愛著我，但我說，在發生了這件事之後，回不去了。

❷ I have to divorce because there can be no going back after what we have been through.
我必須離婚，因為我們在歷經了這一切之後，回不去了。

❸ There can be no going back. Donald Trump has been elected the 45th President of the United States.
回不去了。川普已當選美國第 45 任總統。

★ **remain** [rɪ`men] 動 殘留、仍然、繼續

★ **elect** [ɪ`lɛkt] 動 挑選、選舉／ 形 挑選的

及時行樂

eat, drink, and be merry （動詞）

流行語解密！

這成語的完整寫法是 eat, drink, and be merry, for tomorrow we die，但一般都簡要地寫成 eat, drink, and be merry（亦可寫成 to eat, to drink, and to be merry）。這成語出自聖經中的傳道書 (Ecclesiastes)：A man hath no better thing under the sun, than to eat, and to drink, and to be merry.（人在太陽底下，莫強如吃喝歡樂）。

這樣用就對了！

1. Bill: No cake for me, thank you. I'm on a diet.
   比爾：我不要蛋糕，謝謝。我正在節食。
   Amy: But, Bill, this is a birthday party. Eat, drink, and be merry!
   艾美：但是，比爾，這是生日派對。及時行樂吧！

2. Nina encouraged all her guests to eat, drink, and be merry, for tomorrow we die.
   妮娜鼓勵她的所有客人要及時行樂，因為我們明天就死了。

★ **diet** [ˋdaɪət] 名 飲食／ 動 節食
- ▶ 延伸片語：**be on a diet** 節食
- ▶ 延伸片語：**organic diet** 生機飲食

★ **encourage** [ɪnˋkɝɪdʒ] 動 鼓勵

Track 296

比上不足，比下有餘

In the country of the blind, the one-eyed man is king.

流行語解密！

這句字面的意思是「在盲人的國度裡，有一隻眼睛的人就是國王」。

這樣用就對了！

1. John: How on earth did Michael get promoted to be head of his department? He's such a blunderer!
   約翰：麥可到底是怎樣升到該部門的主管呢？他真的是個粗心大意、常犯錯的人啊！
   Mary: In the country of the blind, the one-eyed man is king.
   瑪麗：比上不足，比下有餘（亦即該部門其他人比他更粗心大意、更常犯錯。）

民粹

populism （名詞）

流行語解密！

民粹（民粹主義）原本是一種代表一般民眾（人民）利益的政治，即平民主義，但在大約 1960 年代之後逐漸通俗、媚俗、粗俗化，成為不肖政客訴諸民眾偏見的政治策略及操弄民眾情緒的工具。以 popul- 為字首的字彙通常有「民眾的……」的意思，例如 population（人口）。另外，就像一般「……主義」ism 的單字一樣，populist（名詞）、（形容詞）是民粹主義者、民粹主義（者）的，而 populistic （形容詞）：民粹的、民粹主義的。

這樣用就對了！

1. The government's ideas are simple populism: tax cuts and higher wages.
   政府的構想全然是民粹：減稅及加薪。

2. The minister accused some legislators of fanning populism.
   這位部長指責一些立法委員操弄民粹。

★ **government** [ˋgʌvənmənt] 名 政府
★ **wage** [wedʒ] 名 薪水
★ **accuse** [əˋkjuz] 動 控告
★ **legislator** [ˋlɛdʒɪsˏletɚ] 名 立法委員
★ **fan** [fæn] 動 煽動

不折不扣

pure and simple（形容詞）

流行語解密！

pure and simple 意為「不折不扣，完全是，純粹是」，都用在它所修飾的名詞（通常為不可數名詞）之後。它的副詞為 purely and simply，意為「不折不扣，完全地，純粹地」。

這樣用就對了！

1. It's blackmail, pure and simple.
   那是不折不扣的敲詐。

2. That murder was vengeance, pure and simple.
   那起謀殺是不折不扣的報復行徑。

3. It's laziness, pure and simple.
   那純粹是懶惰。

4. It was just gossip, pure and simple.
   那純粹是八卦。

5. I lent him $1,000 purely and simply out of friendship.
   我借他一千美元完全是基於友誼。

6. The principal decided to close the library purely and simply because it cost too much to run.
   校長決定關閉圖書館純粹是因為管理費用太高了。

★ **vengeance** [ˋvɛndʒəns] 名 報仇

★ **principle** [ˋprɪnsəpl̩] 名 校長

出洋相；當眾出醜

make an exhibition of oneself （動詞）

流行語解密！

出洋相即是當眾出醜，自不待言。exhibition 是展現的意思，在這裡的展現自己是負面的意思。

這樣用就對了！

1. Whenever Mary sings, she makes an exhibition of herself.
   瑪麗每次唱歌都大出洋相。

2. If Rudy keeps on drinking he's going to end up making an exhibition of himself!
   如果魯迪繼續喝酒，他終將當眾出醜！

再學多一點！

★ **whenever** [hwɛnˋɛvɚ] 連 無論何時／ 副 無論何時

　▶ 同義詞：**anytime** [ˋɛnɪ͵taɪm] 副 任何時候

★ **exhibition** [͵ɛksəˋbɪʃən] 名 展覽會

　▶ 延伸片語：**public exhibition** 名 公開展覽

　▶ 相關詞：**exhibit** [ɪgˋzɪbɪt] 動 展示

★ **keep on** 片 繼續

★ **end up** 片 結果

好人不長命
Those whom the gods love die young.

流行語解密！

英文也可寫成 Whom the gods love die young.，亦有「天妒英才」之意。

這樣用就對了！

1 A: Mr. White died of a heart attack last night. He's just forty-six years old
懷特先生昨晚心臟病發作與世長辭了。他才四十六歲。
B: I'm so sorry to hear that. He's one of the greatest philanthropists in the world. Those whom the gods love die young.
我聽了這消息很難過。他是全世界最偉大的慈善家之一。好人不長命。

2 So many brilliant authors and artists died before the age of fifty that it's easy to believe that those whom the gods love die young.
許多傑出的作家和藝術家不到五十歲就撒手人寰了，讓人不由得地相信天妒英才。

再學多一點！

★ **heart attack** 片 心臟病
▶ 相關詞：**attack** [əˋtæk] 動 攻擊
★ **philanthropist** [fɪˋlænθrəpɪst] 名 慈善家
★ **brilliant** [ˋbrɪljənt] 形 閃耀的
★ **author** [ˋɔθɚ] 名 作者

老樣子

same old, same old（名詞）

流行語解密！

中文的「老套；老掉牙；千篇一律」亦可用 (the) same old, same old 這一美國口語來表示。有人認為它是從同義片語 “the same old thing” 衍生而來；有時亦寫成 same old same old。

這樣用就對了！

1. A: How are things at work? / How's work going?
   工作情況怎麼樣？
   B: Oh, same old, same old.
   哦，老樣子。

2. The same old same old! The rich get richer and the poor get poorer.
   老套了！富者越富、貧者越貧。

3. I just keep on doing the same old, same old every day and soon I'm going to die of boredom!
   我每天都千篇一律做同樣的事情，不了多久我將因無聊而死！

4. John gets tired of eating the same old thing for breakfast.
   約翰厭倦早餐都吃同樣的東西。

老梗

such a cliché!（片語）

流行語解密！

我們還可使用 old chestnut 來表達相同的意思。cliché 是個從法文而來的字，意為「陳腔濫調；陳腐的說法」，而 old chestnut 意為「陳腐的故事；老掉牙的笑話」。

這樣用就對了！

❶ It's all such a cliché!
那完全是老梗了！

❷ Not that old chestnut again!
別再講那個老掉牙的笑話了！／別再老梗了！

多往好的方面想；多往好處想

count one's blessings （動詞）

流行語解密！

這句話直譯是「細數自己的幸福」，也就是往好的方面想。凡事多往好的方面想，內心自然豁然開朗，生活將充滿希望。

這樣用就對了！

1. School children today should count their blessings. At least they're not beaten for talking in class as we were.
現今的學童應該多往好的方面想。至少他們在課堂上講話不會像我們以前那樣被打。

2. Daniel wanted to leave his job a year ago. Then he started to count his blessings. He has a comfortable apartment and a lot of good friends.
丹尼爾一年前曾想辭去他的工作，但後來他往好的方面想，他有一間舒適的公寓和許多好朋友。

★ **at least** 片 至少

★ **comfortable** [ˋkʌmfətəbḷ] 形 舒服的

★ **apartment** [əˋpɑrtmənt] 名 公寓

▶ 延伸片語：**garden apartment** 名 花園公寓

▶ 同義詞：**flat** [flæt] 名 公寓

有過之而無不及

in spades （片語）

流行語解密！

這片語還意為「非常；極度；大量」(to a great degree, in large amount)。

這樣用就對了！

1. He complained that Allen had stolen some of his ideas, but Randy didn't mention that he had done the same in spades.
他抱怨艾倫竊取了他的一些構想，但蘭迪並未提及他也竊取別人的構想，有過之而無不及。

2. All the workers may think the old boss was bad-tempered, but the new one is the same—in spades!
所有員工可能都認為舊老闆脾氣暴躁，但新老闆的脾氣也一樣，有過之而無不及！

再學多一點！

★ **complain** [kəm`plen] 動 抱怨
▶ 延伸片語：**complain about...** 抱怨……

★ **steal** [stil] 動 偷、騙取
▶ 動詞變化：**steal-stole-stolen**
▶ 延伸片語：**steal from...** 從……中偷走

★ **mention** [`mɛnʃən] 動 提起／名 提及
▶ 延伸片語：**mention of...** 提及……

★ **temper** [`tɛmpɚ] 名 脾氣
▶ 延伸片語：**lose one's temper** 發脾氣

自欺欺人；鴕鳥心態
bury one's head in the sand （動詞）

流行語解密！

動詞 bury 可用 hide 來代替。

這樣用就對了！

1. Stop burying your head in the sand. Look at the statistics on smoking and cancer.
別再自欺欺人了。看看這些有關抽菸與癌症的統計數字吧。

2. Parents said bullying was being ignored, and accused the headmaster of burying his head in the sand.
家長表示，霸凌問題遭到漠視，並譴責校長採取鴕鳥心態。

束手無策；無計可施；黔驢技窮
at one's wits' end（成語）

亦可寫成 at one's wit's end。

這樣用就對了！

1. I'm at my wits' end with this problem.
我對這問題無計可施。

② I have a problem that has me at wits' end, and I'm hoping you can help.
我有個問題使我束手無策，我期望你能幫忙。

見好就收

quit while one is ahead （動詞）

流行語解密！

quit 的動詞三態為 quit, quit, quit 或 (英) quit, quitted, quitted，而現在分詞為 quitting。

這樣用就對了！

① When will you consider quitting while you're ahead?
你什麼時候才會考慮見好就收呢？

② When we won a thousand dollars at the casino, we quit while we were ahead.
我們在賭場贏了一千美元之後，我們見好就收。

★ **consider** [kən`sɪdɚ] 動 仔細考慮

▶ 延伸片語：**consider... as...** 認為……是……

▶ 相關詞：**considerable** [kən`sɪdərəbl̩] 形 應考慮的、相當多
consideration [kən͵sɪdə`reʃən] 名 考慮

★ **casino** [kə`sino] 名 賭場

活到老學到老

live and learn （動詞）

流行語解密！

用於表示對剛知道的新事物感到驚訝。也可以說 It's never too late to learn.（學習永不嫌晚）。

這樣用就對了！

1. I had no idea that she was as old as that. Well, you live and learn.
   我沒想到她年紀這麼大了。真是活到老學到老。

2. I didn't know that snakes could swim. Well, live and learn!
   我以前不知道蛇會游泳。真是活到老學到老！

看熱鬧

rubberneck （動詞）

這個字是伸長脖子看的意思，亦可當名詞用，意為「看熱鬧的人」，可能是觀望的人，或是觀光客因為好奇而伸長脖子看。

這樣用就對了！

1. If these people would stop rubbernecking, we could drive past them.
   如果這些人不要再看熱鬧，我們的車子就可以通過了。

❷ The traffic jam was caused by rubbernecks.
交通擁塞是由看熱鬧的人所造成。

風水輪流轉

Every dog has its day.（成語）

流行語解密！

亦可用 every dog has his day. 來表示。另外有一句類似的是 Every cloud has a silver lining.（每朵雲都鑲著銀邊。）烏雲是厄運的意思，鑲著銀色的邊則是好運的意思，所以這句話是壞運結束後會有好運，也就是否極泰來的意思。

這樣用就對了！

❶ I believe you'll get chosen for the basketball team. Every dog has its day.
我相信你會獲選加入籃球隊。風水輪流轉。

❷ You may become successful someday. Every dog has his day.
有朝一日你可能會成功。風水輪流轉。

★ **sliver** [ˋslɪvɚ] 形 銀色的
★ **lining** [ˋlaɪnɪŋ] 名 內襯
★ **successful** [səkˋsɛsfəl] 形 成功的

恕難同意

beg to differ (vi.) (with+ 受詞)

流行語解密！

beg to differ 的主詞都是 I。這動詞片語亦可表示「恕難從命」、「恕難照辦」的意思。

這樣用就對了！

1. John: Opera is way better than Firefox.
   約翰：Opera 比 Firefox 好很多。
   Mary: I beg to differ; you can customize Firefox just the way you want.
   瑪麗：我恕難同意；你可以將 Firefox 自訂成你想要的樣子。

2. I beg to differ with Professor Lee's final assertion.
   我恕難同意李教授最後的聲明。

★ **beg** [bɛg] 動 乞討、懇求
▶ 延伸片語：**beg for** 乞求

★ **differ** [ˋdɪfɚ] 動 不同、相異
▶ 延伸片語：**differ with...** 與……不同
▶ 相關詞：**different** [ˋdɪfərənt] 形 不同於（+ from）

★ **customize** [ˋkʌstəm͵aɪz] 動 客製化
▶ 相關詞：**customer** [ˋkʌstəmɚ] 名 顧客、客戶

★ **assertion** [əˋsɝʃən] 名 申明
▶ 相關詞：**assert** [əˋsɝt] 動 堅信

站在正義的一方

on the side of the angels (idiom)

流行語解密！

這成語是兩度擔任英國首相的保守黨政治家班傑明·迪斯雷利 (Benjamin Disraeli)1864 年在牛津大學發表一篇有關達爾文 (Charles Darwin 1809-1882) 進化論的演說時所創的。當時他說："The question is this: Is man an ape or an angel? I, my Lord, am on the side of the angels."（問題是：人究竟是猴子，還是天使呢？主啊，我站在天使這一邊）。

這樣用就對了！

1. I am always on the side of the angels.
   我永遠站在正義的一方。

2. Kent was on the side of the angels even though it was neither profitable nor popular.
   即使無利可圖且不孚眾望，肯特仍站在正義的一方。

★ **ape** [ep] 名 猿

★ **profitable** [ˋprɑfɪtəbḷ] 形 有利的

▶ 同義詞：**beneficial** [ˏbɛnəˋfɪʃəl] 有利的

★ **profit** [ˋprɑfɪt] 名 利益

★ **the theory of evolution** 進化論

▶ 相關詞：**theory** [ˋθiərɪ] 名 理論

▶ 相關詞：**evolution** [ˏɛvəˋluʃən] 名 進化

說一套，做一套

talk the talk, but not walk the walk （動詞）

流行語解密！

第一個 talk 和 walk 是動詞，第二個 talk 和 walk 為名詞。與 “Talk is cheap.”（說說而已）的意思大致相同。

這樣用就對了！

1. When it comes to recycling he talks the talk but he doesn't walk the walk.
   談到資源回收，他是說一套，做一套。

2. Tom often talks the talk but he doesn't walk the walk.
   湯姆經常說一套，做一套。

造化弄人；命運的捉弄；命運的安排

(by) a quirk of fate （名詞）

流行語解密！

這片語的前面往往加上介系詞 by 來構成副詞片語。

這樣用就對了！

1. A quirk of fate led her to work in the US and die in an uncanny car accident.
造化弄人，使她到美國工作而死於一場離奇的車禍中。

2. By a quirk of fate the couple booked into the same hotel after years of being apart.
命運的安排讓這對失散多年的戀人住進同一家旅館。

★ **quirk** [ˋkwɝk] 名 突然轉變，花體字

★ **fate** [fet] 名 命運、宿命

▶ 延伸片語：**man is the master of his own fate** 人定勝天

★ **uncanny** [ʌnˋkænɪ] 形 奇怪的，可怕的

★ **book into** 入住

★ **apart** [əˋpart] 副 分開

▶ 延伸片語：**apart from...** 除開、除……之外

該到的都到了；該來的都來了

all present and accounted for（美）；all present and correct（英）（片語）

流行語解密！

按理說，這裡的 and 應改為 or，但口語都是這樣用，這片語可指人或事物。

這樣用就對了！

1. Is everyone ready to run the marathon? All present and accounted for.
   每個人都準備好跑馬拉松了嗎？該來的都來了。

2. Are all the students here? Nearly all present and correct.
   所有學生都到了嗎？該到的幾乎都到了。

跟自己過不去

cut off one's nose to spite one's face （動詞）

流行語解密！

這句英文也在表示「把氣出在自己身上」的意思，其中 spite 這個動詞意為「存心刁難；故意激怒」，通常接在 to 的後面。

這樣用就對了！

1. John: The next time he treats me like that, I'm just going to quit my job.
   約翰：下次如果他再那樣對我，我就要辭職了。
   Mary: Isn't that a bit like cutting off your nose to spite your face?
   瑪麗：那不是有點像跟自己過不去嗎？

2. If you stay home because your ex-husband will be at the party, aren't you just cutting off your nose to spite your face?
   如果妳因為妳前夫會參加派對而留在家裡，那麼妳不就是跟自己過不去嗎？

★ **spite** [spaɪt] 名 惡意

★ **treat** [trit] 動 對待

▶ 相關詞：**treatment** [tritmənt] 名 款待

Chapter 14

鄉民都在說什麼？

低頭族

phubber（名詞）[ˋfʌbɚ]

流行語解密！

這個字是由 phone（手機）+ snubber（冷落他人者）組合而成。其動詞為 phub，意為「在社交場合只顧著低頭玩手機而冷落朋友」，而 phubbing 為現在分詞或動名詞，意為「在社交場合只顧著低頭玩手機而冷落朋友的行徑」。這幾個新字目前都還未被字典所收錄，但已被全球各大英文新聞媒體廣泛採用。

這樣用就對了！

1. The number of phubbers has risen dramatically in recent years.
最近幾年低頭族的人數急遽增加。

2. Phubbing is a growing modern social scourge.
低頭玩手機不理會他人的行徑，是現代社交一項越來越嚴重的禍害。

★ **dramatically** [drəˋmætɪklɪ] 副 戲劇般的

★ **recent** [rɪˋzɛnt] 形 最近的

▶ 延伸片語：**in recent years** 近幾年

★ **social** [ˋsoʃəl] 形 社會的

★ **scourge** [skɝdʒ] 名 災禍

懶人包

for dummies（名詞）

流行語解密！

「懶人包」沒有固定英文，也鮮少單獨使用，通常以「……懶人包」的形式出現，如「服貿協議懶人包」。For dummies (or FOR DUMMIES, For Dummies) 是當今世界最暢銷的教學 / 自學或參考系列叢書 (instructional/reference books)，由美國 John Wiley & Sons（前稱 IDG Books / Hungry Minds）公司出版；它也是全球著名的品牌之一，在國外，尤其是在英語系國家，可謂家喻戶曉。《紐約時報》曾將之譽為「不僅是出版現象，更是時代標誌！」

自 1991 年 11 月第一本 FOR DUMMIES 書籍（一本教人如何使用 DOS 作業系統的書籍，名叫 "DOS FOR DUMMIES"）出版以來，迄今此系列叢書已出版了 1,800 多種書目，從運動到歷史、從音樂到數學、從電腦到 DIY、從美食到旅遊等各個方面都有，被翻譯成 30 多種語言，全球發行總量超過兩億五千萬冊。FOR DUMMIES 系列叢書，內容皆經主題領域專家有系統地整理，深入淺出地將知識理論以最簡單的文字、搭配一目了然的表格與圖片介紹給讀者，易學易懂。

根據上述，再加上 FOR DUMMIES 亦鮮少單獨使用，通常以「... for dummies」的形式出現，如 Acne For Dummies, Fishing For Dummies，懶人包的英文不就是 for dummies 嗎，Bingo!。

這樣用就對了！

1. A book called "English Idioms FOR DUMMIES" is expected to be put out next month.
   一本名叫《英文成語懶人包》的書將在下月出版。

2. You can find a lot of grammar and other English-learning for dummies e-books on the Internet.
   你可在網路上找到許多文法及其他英文學習的懶人包電子書。

網路爆紅

Internet sensation（名詞）；go viral（動詞）

流行語解密！

這兩個片語通常用來指影片、圖片、音樂或笑話在網路上被許多網友點閱或觀看。

這樣用就對了！

1. A video of four youngsters dancing on a rainy street corner has become an Internet sensation.
   = A video of four youngsters dancing on a rainy street corner has gone viral.
   一支顯示四個青少年雨中街頭跳舞的影片在網路上爆紅。

2. After the video became an Internet sensation, visitors to our blog doubled overnight.
   = After the video went viral, visitors to our blog doubled overnight.
   那段影片在網路上爆紅之後，我們部落格的點閱人數一夜間暴增一倍。

★ **sensation** [sɛnˋseʃən] 名 感覺
★ **viral** [ˋvaɪrəl] 形 像病毒一樣廣為流傳，病毒（引起）的
★ **youngster** [ˋjʌŋstɚ] 名 年輕人
★ **overnight** [ˋovɚˋnaɪt] 形 徹夜的、過夜的／副 整夜地

Track 320

鄉民／網友／網民／婉君

netizen（名詞）

流行語解密！

婉君原為 PTT 上的用語，是「網軍」的諧音，現在一般媒體也使用這個詞，使其成為頗夯的流行語。不過，其他名稱，如網友、網民、鄉民，亦都可用 netizen 來表示。這個字是由 net 與 citizen 組合而成，於 1984 年首次被使用，現已被《牛津英語大辭典》(Oxford English Dictionary, OED) 所收錄。

這樣用就對了！

1. The ruling party underestimated the strength of netizens' feelings on this issue.
   執政黨低估了婉君關注這個問題的強烈程度。

2. The number of rural netizens in China is growing dramatically.
   中國農村婉君人數正急遽增加。

再學多一點！

★ **ruling** [rulɪŋ] 形 統治的

★ **party** [ˋpɑrtɪ] 名 黨派、派對

▶ 延伸片語：**be party to sth.** 支持，參加……

★ **underestimate** [ˋʌndɚˋɛstəmɪt] 動 低估

▶ 相關詞：**estimate** [ˋɛstəmɪt] 名 評估／動 評估

★ **strength** [strɛŋθ] 名 力量

★ **rural** [ˋrʊrəl] 形 農村的

酸民

hater(s)（名詞）

流行語解密！

常會有人在無地放矢的嗆人，或是不分青紅皂白就先嗆人，這些總是在「酸」人的鄉「民」被稱作「酸民」。在英文中稱作 hater，也就是 hate（憎恨）＋ -er（的人）。這詞常加上 -s，因為酸民通常不只一個。之前也曾經在各大社群網站流傳「黑特」一詞，主要是匿名表達對於某些人的不滿，也是取自英文 hater 一詞。

這樣用就對了！

1. That the haters keep condemning his mistakes makes him crazy.
酸民一直酸他的錯誤讓他快瘋了。

2. Just ignore the response from a hater.
不要理會酸民的回應。

Track 322

網路男蟲或女蟲

catfish（名詞）

流行語解密！

這個詞源自美國 2010 年一部名為 “Catfish” 的紀錄片。” Catfish” 在台灣的中文片名叫做《非識不可》(Facebook)，大陸則直譯為《鯰魚》。網路男蟲或女蟲是指用假帳號在網路上騙財騙色的人。

這樣用就對了！

1. Many guys have multiple accounts on Facebook because they are catfishes.
許多傢伙都有多個臉書帳號，一人分飾多角，因為他們是網路男蟲。

2. I was really falling for that gorgeous gal on Facebook, but she turned out to be a catfish.
我真的很喜歡臉書上那個美眉，但她竟然是個網路女蟲。

亂碼

garbled code （名詞）

流行語解密！

garbled 為形容詞，意為「含混不清的；搞亂了的」。

這樣用就對了！

1. Why do my PDFs open in garbled code?
我的 PDF 文件為什麼開起來都是亂碼呢？

2. The Wordpress plugin caused my blog to show garbled code.
這個 Wordpress 外掛造成我的部落格顯示亂碼。

★ **cause** [kɔz] 動 造成

網路用語／火星文
Internet slang（名詞）

流行語解密！

Internet slang 的意思是網路用語，也有人把它翻作「火星文」。火星文這一名稱最早出現於台灣社會，隨即流行到香港、中國大陸和海外華人社會，指的是以青少年為主的網友或網民，在社群網站、即時通訊和簡訊中使用的網路語言，除 Internet slang 外，還有數個字詞可以表達「火星文」的意思，包括 Internet shorthand、netspeak 和 chatspeak。

這樣用就對了！

1. LOL is an abbreviation for “laughing out loud” or “laugh out loud” used in Internet slang.
   LOL 在網路用語中是 laughing out loud 或 laugh out loud 的縮寫 — 「大笑」。

2. LTNS: “long time no see” — Internet slang.
   LTNS 在火星文中是表示 long time no see －「好久不見」。

Track 325

狂
savage（名詞）

流行語解密！

這是在網路上興起的詞，用來說人事物非常的酷，非常瘋狂，後來也有 948794 狂（就是白痴就是狂）的用法。在英文會用 savage（野蠻），這個字可以當名詞，形容詞或是動詞使用。

這樣用就對了！

1. The monk who talked about karma is savage! He said you should feel it's your eye's karma to see your husband has an affair.
那討論業障的法師真的太狂了！他竟然說看到你丈夫外遇要覺得是你眼睛業障重。

2. You are going to Paris for the bag? That's savage.
你去巴黎就只是為了買那個包？太狂了。

Track 326

請私訊我

DM (direct message) （動詞）

流行語解密！

近年來流行的網路用語，常常會看到臉書等網路平台上有人要詢問商品細節，商家回覆是 DM 表示請私訊我。在中文也很常看到有人在下面留言回覆「已私」代表已經傳過訊息了，請注意這則訊息。

這樣用就對了！

1. I think this dress is pretty. I will DM the seller.
我覺得這件洋裝很漂亮，我要私訊賣家。

2. She seems to be upset, so I DMed her.
她看起來很難過，所以我私訊她了。

Chapter 15 吃喝拉撒睡！

吃貨

foodaholic（名詞）

流行語解密！

這個字是由 food（食物）＋ alcoholic（酒精）所組成的，指的是很愛吃東西的人，也就是中文的「吃貨」。如果是只喜歡吃美食，則是 foodie（饕客），若是專業的美食評論家則是 gourmet，gourmet 也可以當形容詞形容食物美味的。

這樣用就對了！

1. Since your girlfriend is such a foodaholic, you can make her very happy simply by bringing her some food.
既然你女朋友是這樣的吃貨，你只需要帶點食物給她就可以讓她很開心了。

2. When foodies visit Thailand, they must try Thai food.
饕客們到了泰國一定會嘗試泰式料理。

Track 328

空腹

on an empty stomach（片語）

流行語解密！

an empty stomach 是「空著肚子」的意思，要注意的是，在句子中使用這片語時，前面要加介系詞 on。此外，英文中由 stomach 所構成的慣用語不在少數，例如：have/get butterflies in one's stomach（緊張不安、心神不寧）也是其中之一。

這樣用就對了！

1. You should avoid drinking alcohol on an empty stomach.
   你應該避免空腹喝酒。

2. Jeff left early this morning and drove three hours on an empty stomach.
   傑夫今晨一早就出發，空著肚子開了三小時的車。

Track 329

你有口臭／體臭

You got the dragon/ B.O.

流行語解密！

口臭最常用的是 bad breath（不好的氣味），也可以說 dragon breath，而 dragon breath 除了口臭還可以指天冷吐氣時冒的白煙。至於體味則是用 B.O.(body order)，如果說人家體味很重，或是有體臭，都是用 strong（強烈的）來形容，如果用 horrible（可怕的）來形容，則是非常可怕的體味。

這樣用就對了！

1. You got the dragon today.
   你今天有口臭。

2. Dude, go brush your teeth! You got the dragon.
   老兄，快去刷牙，你有口臭。

3. I do not have horrible B.O.!
   我沒有難聞的體臭！

4. Gary had such strong B.O. that I almost passed out.
   蓋瑞的體臭難聞到我差點昏過去。

擤鼻涕

blow one's nose （動詞）

流行語解密！

blow 是「吹」的意思，因為擤鼻涕時就像是吹鼻子。而流鼻涕的英文叫做 someone's nose is running 或 someone has a runny nose。

這樣用就對了！

1. Excuse me, I have to blow my nose because I am seriously sick.
   對不起，我得去擤個鼻涕因為我生重病。

2. Irving blew his nose into his handkerchief.
   歐文把鼻涕擤在手帕上。

Track 331

挖鼻孔

pick one's nose （動詞）

流行語解密！

名詞是 nose-picking，例如：Nose-picking in public is an action condemned in many culture.（在許多文化中，公開挖鼻孔的行為都會被譴責。）鼻屎的英文叫做 booger，鼻涕叫做 (nasal) mucus 或 snot（不雅的說法）。

這樣用就對了！

1. Stop picking your nose!
別挖鼻孔！

2. Don't pick your nose in public!
別當眾挖鼻孔。

Track 332

激凸

camel toe（名詞）; moose knuckle（名詞）

流行語解密！

Camel toe 指的是女性穿著緊身褲或所穿的褲子太緊以致於私處顯示在外的形狀，就像駱駝的腳趾一樣。至於 moose knuckle，就是男性的激凸，即男性穿著緊身褲或所穿的褲子太緊以致於私處顯示在外的形狀，亦叫做 male camel toe一女性的激凸是否也可以叫做 female moose knuckle? 似乎不行。有趣的是，男性也是用動物的身體部位來比擬，其形狀有如北美麋鹿的蹄。

這樣用就對了！

1. Should I tell the girl about her camel toe?
我該告訴那女孩她激凸了嗎？

2. I was walking down the street and saw a man in tight jeans with a wicked moose knuckle!
我走在街上時看到一位穿著緊身牛仔褲、激凸得很厲害的男子！

雞皮疙瘩

goose bumps or goosebumps; goose pimples; gooseflesh （名詞）

流行語解密！

（因寒冷、害怕或興奮而）起雞皮疙瘩，英文叫做 have/get goose bumps，而使人起雞皮疙瘩叫做 give someone goose bumps；至於「雞皮疙瘩掉滿地」，則是 a lot of goosebumps。

這樣用就對了！

1. Whenever I hear that old song, I get goose bumps.
   每當我聽到那首老歌，我都會起雞皮疙瘩。

2. I never have goose pimples, but my teeth chatter when it's cold.
   我從未起雞皮疙瘩，但天氣寒冷時，我的牙齒會打哆嗦。

3. Mr. Chen and his wife called each other by cutesy pet names that gave me a lot of goosebumps.
   陳先生和他太太互以肉麻的寵物名字稱呼對方，讓我雞皮疙瘩掉滿地。

★ **goose pimples** 片 雞皮疙瘩
  ▶相關詞：**pimple** [ˋpɪmpl̩] 名 青春痘

★ **goose flesh** 片 （小）雞皮疙瘩

★ **cutesy** [kjutsɪ] 形 造作的，裝可愛的

Track 334

汗流浹背；揮汗如雨；滿身大汗

sweat like a pig （動詞）

流行語解密！

像豬一樣流汗，就是汗流浹背的意思囉！亦可用 to sweat bullets 來表達相同的意思，亦即因出力、恐懼、緊張或焦慮而全身冒汗。

這樣用就對了！

1. That was really good exercise. I'm sweating like a pig!
   那真是不錯的運動。我已經汗流浹背了！

2. Kelly was so frightened that she was sweating like a pig.
   凱莉嚇得滿身大汗。

3. Jerry was sweating bullets when the teacher questioned him.
   當老師質問他的時候，傑瑞已經揮汗如雨了。

再學多一點！

★ **bullet** [ˋbʊlɪt] 名 子彈

★ **frightened** [ˋfraɪtn̩d] 形 害怕的

★ **question** [ˋkwɛstʃən] 動 質疑、懷疑

▶ 延伸片語：**in question** 正在討論的

▶ 延伸片語：**come into question** 成為問題

大姨媽

Aunt Flo（名詞）

流行語解密！

雖然英文的月經 menstrual period 說法不下 10 種之多，最正式的說法是 be on a period/have a period（生理期），但以 Aunt Flo 來表示「大姨媽」最為傳神。

這樣用就對了！

1. My Aunt Flo will visit next week.
   我的大姨媽下週會來。

2. Aunt Flo arrived yesterday.
   大姨媽昨天來了。

Track 336

美容覺

beauty sleep（名詞）

流行語解密！

beauty sleep 就是可讓一個人保持健康、心情愉悅，看起來容光煥發、神采奕奕的足夠睡眠，通常位在動詞 get 或 need 之後。

這樣用就對了！

1. I'm too tired, so I want to go home right now to get some beauty sleep.
   我太累了，所以我想要馬上回家睡個美容覺。

2 You are always beautiful! Cindy, you don't need some beauty sleep.
妳一向美麗動人。辛蒂，妳不需要美容覺。

3 My wife is usually in bed long before midnight—she needs her beauty sleep.
我太太通常早在半夜之前就已就寢了—她需要足夠的睡眠。

睡懶覺

sleep in （動詞）

流行語解密！

這個片語動詞就是表示「晚起床」的意思。另外 sleep in 也有睡過頭的意思，也可能是睡在工作的地方。

這樣用就對了！

1 Let's sleep in tomorrow morning—we haven't had a chance for a long time.
明天早上我們就睡懶覺吧—我們好久都沒有這樣的機會。

2 The whole family sleeps in on Sundays.
全家人星期天都睡懶覺。

★跟 sleep 有關的搭配用法：

sleep off/away 睡一覺（疼痛）就會消失了

sleep with 跟（某人）睡覺，跟（某人）上床

恍神

brain fart（名詞）

流行語解密！

brain fart 字面意思為「腦子放屁」。舉凡心不在焉、突然忘記某事、突然忘了做某事或做過某事、不經意地說出原本不該說或不想說的話，以及其他類似的情況，都是 brain fart 所產生的結果。

這樣用就對了！

1. What did the teacher say? I just had a brain fart.
   老師說了什麼？我剛剛恍神了一下。

2. I just had a brain fart. Damn! What's your idea?
   我剛剛恍神了一下。該死！你可以再說一次你的想法嗎？

Track 339

被自己的屁驚醒／嚇到

puppy fart syndrome（名詞）

流行語解密！

顯然地，只有放大屁（huge fart）或響屁（loud fart）才會有這樣的效果。

這樣用就對了！

1. Puppy fart syndrome can probably happen to us all.
我們每個人都可能被自己的屁嚇到。

2. When I was just drifting off to sleep, I let out a loud fart and woke up. This is so-called puppy fart syndrome.
我剛要入睡時突然放了個響屁，然後就驚醒了。這就是所謂的被屁嚇醒。

鬧鐘叫不醒

sleep through the alarm （動詞）

流行語解密！

片語動詞 sleep through (something) 意為「睡著沒被（某事物）吵醒」。對於習慣晚睡或不習慣早起的人，鬧鐘往往發揮不了作用。「習慣早起的人」叫做 morning person，例如：I am not a morning person.（我不是個習慣早起的人。）

這樣用就對了！

1. If I'm really sleepy, I'll just sleep through the alarm!
如果我真的很睏，連鬧鐘都叫不醒的！

2. Brenda didn't hear the storm last night. She must have slept through it.
布蘭達昨晚沒有聽見暴風雨的聲音。她肯定睡得太熟了。

起床氣

get out on the wrong side of the bed （動詞）

流行語解密！

這兩個成語是美國、英國和澳洲共通的講法，但美國還使用 to get up on the wrong side of the bed 來表達相同的意思，即「（早上一起床就）心情不好」，也就是「起床氣」。

這樣用就對了！

1. Why are you shouting at me? Did you get out on bed on the wrong side?
   你幹麼一直兇我？你有起床氣嗎？

2. A: Why are you getting mad at me? Didn't I do anything wrong?
   你幹嘛對我發脾氣啊？我做錯了什麼嗎？
   B：Sorry, I got out on the wrong side of the bed.
   對不起，我有起床氣。

補眠

catch up on some Zs （動詞）

流行語解密！

我們亦可用 get some shut-eye 來表達相同的意思；shut-eye 字面上的意思是眼睛合起來，在口語上是「睡覺；睡眠」的意思。

這樣用就對了！

❶ I need to catch up on some Zs.
我需要補個眠。

❷ Who doesn't need to get some shut-eye?
誰不需要補眠呢？

Track 343

落枕

get/have a crick in one's neck （動詞）

流行語解密！

crick 意為「扭傷」，可當名詞和動詞用。
To get/have a crick in one's neck 字面意思為「頸部扭傷」。若將動詞 get/have 拿掉，則 a crick in one's neck 就變成了名詞。

這樣用就對了！

❶ I got a crick in my neck from sleeping on a mat yesterday.
我昨天睡在墊子上而造成落枕。

❷ John read on the plane and had a crick in his neck the other day.
約翰幾天前在飛機上看書，結果落枕。

再學多一點！

★ **crick** [krɪk] 動（背部頸部的）痛，痙攣

★ **mat** [mæt] 名 墊子、席子

▶ 相關詞：**carpet** 名 地毯

▶ 相關詞：**rug** 名 毯子

音癡

tone-deaf（形容詞）

流行語解密！

tone 意思是曲調，tone-deaf 字面上意思是「曲調的聾子」也就是俗稱的「音癡」。相反地，如果要說人音準很準的話可以用 can carry a tune，這邊的 tune 也意為「曲調」，除 carry 外，tune 還可與其他動詞連用來表達其他的意思，例如：play/hum/sing/whistle a tune（彈／哼／唱／用口哨吹曲子）。

這樣用就對了！

1. A: Can you carry a tune?
   你唱歌好聽嗎？
   B: No, I'm tone-deaf. I can just hum a tune.
   不好聽，我五音不全。我只能哼哼曲子。

2. Mary could carry a tune very well. I always enjoyed hearing her singing.
   瑪麗唱歌很好聽。我一直很喜歡聽她唱歌。

★ **tone** [ton] 名 風格、音調
　▶ 延伸片語：**set the tone** 說了算

★ **deaf** [dɛf] 形 耳聾
　▶ 延伸片語：**turn a deaf ear to...** 對……充耳不聞

★ **tune** [tjun] 名 調子、曲調／動 調整音調
　▶ 延伸片語：**out of tune** 走調

★ **hum** [hʌm] 動 哼

★ **whistle** [ˋhwɪsḷ] 動 吹口哨

Track 345

嘴炮／打屁

shoot the breeze （動詞）

流行語解密！

（打）嘴炮是說人鬼扯。英文是 shoot the breeze，亦可用 shoot the bull 或是 throw the bull、throw the crap 來表示完全相同的意思，即「打屁，閒聊，閒扯，瞎扯」。不過這用法比較粗鄙，要注意使用的場合喔！

這樣用就對了！

1. We usually shoot the breeze.
   我們經常聊天打屁。

2. They're just shooting the bull.
   他們只是在打嘴炮。

Chapter 16

這個最夯，講了就不乾！

最夯／超夯／很夯

be (all) the rage（動詞）

流行語解密！

紅極一時的東西，也就是很「夯」。在英文中，rage 含有狂熱席捲的意含，也可以用來形容席捲各地的流行，如果說人事物 be all the rage 則是「很夯」的意思。

這樣用就對了！

1. The Korean soap opera was all the rage. But no one cares about it now.
   那部韓劇曾經很夯，可是現在也沒人在討論了。

2. Have you tried this cake? It is the rage now!
   你吃過這個蛋糕嗎？它現在超夯的！

Track 347

廢到笑

funny crap（名詞）

流行語解密！

在網路也很常用「廢到笑」這個詞，用來形容影片等東西非常沒有意義、很「廢」，但是卻能莫名戳重笑點。crap 是「胡扯」、「拉屎」的意思，但是加上了 funny 就是很鬼扯但又很好笑的「廢到笑」。如果在網路或是 youtube 上搜尋 funny crap，出現的「廢到笑」一定會讓你印象深刻吧！

這樣用就對了！

1. I downloaded many funny crap images to reply to my friends' status anytime.
我下載很多廢到笑的圖片用來隨時回覆我朋友的動態。

2. My friend sent me a funny crap video which made me burst out laughing in the class.
我朋友傳給我一個廢到笑的影片，害我上課時不小心噴笑。

Track 348

（講話／食物）很乾

(as) dry as dust（片語）

流行語解密！

中文說人講話很乾，意思是很無聊、不知道要說什麼。在英文也有一句 (as) dry as dust 本意是跟灰塵一樣乾，可以具體地形容食物或其他物品的濕度不足，或是形容人事物很「枯燥乏味」，也就是我們說的「很乾」。

這樣用就對了！

1. Having dinner with my parents-in-law, I felt I was as dry as dust.
跟我公婆吃飯的時候，我覺得很乾。

2. The bread is as dry as dust.
這麵包味同嚼蠟。

3. Because I've been playing the mobile game all day long, my eyes are as dry as dust.
一整天都在玩手遊，我覺得我的眼睛超乾的。

入口即化

melt in one's mouth（動詞）

但"butter would not melt in one's mouth"可不是「奶油不會入口即化」，而是「道貌岸然」的意思。

這樣用就對了！

1. These chocolates somewhat melt in your mouth.
這些巧克力真的能入口即化。

2. These quality ice creams really melt in your mouth.
這些高級冰淇淋真的入口即化。

沒這屁股就不要吃這瀉藥／怕熱就不要進廚房

If you can't stand the heat, get out of the kitchen.

流行語
解密！

閩南語中有一句諺語「沒這屁股就不要吃這瀉藥」，意思是說人如果沒有這種本事就不要做這種（大）事情，跟英文的「怕熱就不要進廚房」有異曲同工的意思。大多數人都認為"If you

can't stand the heat, get out of the kitchen." 是密蘇里州出生的美國前總統杜魯門 (Harry S. Truman, 1884-1972，在位 1945-1953) 講的，其實不然。他曾在一次談話中指出，"If you can't stand the heat, get out of the kitchen" 的「原創者」是密蘇里州傑克森郡 (Jackson County, Missouri) 法院的法官巴克 ‧ 柏塞爾 (Buck Purcell)，只是經由他的嘴巴講出而變得家喻戶曉、眾所周知。這句諺語經常被縮略為 If you can't stand the heat，因為一般都認為聽者只要聽到前半部，就知道後半部了。現今許多英文諺語或俗話亦以這樣的方式來表達，因為它們廣為人知，說話者只要講出各該諺語的前半部，聽者就瞭解意思了。

這樣用就對了！

1. Ted: I didn't think being an engineer could be so stressful.
   泰德：我沒有想到，當工程師，壓力會這麼大。
   Todd: If you can't stand the heat, get out of the kitchen.
   陶德：怕熱就不要進廚房。

2. Maria: This course is too tough; the teacher should let us slow down a bit.
   瑪麗亞：這課程太難了；老師應該讓我們放鬆點。
   Marcia: If you can't stand the heat, get out of the kitchen.
   瑪西亞：怕熱就別進廚房。

★ **engineer** [ˌɛndʒəˋnɪr] 名 工程師

★ **stress** [strɛs] 名 壓力╱ 動 強調、著重

★ **course** [kors] 名 課程、講座、過程、路線

▶ 延伸片語：**in the course of...** 在……過程中

浪子回頭

the return of the prodigal son（名詞）

流行語解密！

the prodigal son 意為「浪子」，源自聖經中浪子回頭的故事。Prodigal 當形容詞時意為「浪費的；揮霍的；奢侈的」，但它亦可當名詞用，意思就是「浪子」。

這樣用就對了！

1. The Smith family saw the return of the prodigal son last night with Steve once again in the family after five years away.
史密斯一家人昨晚將迎接浪子回頭，因為史蒂夫在離家五年後將重返這個家庭。

2. So, the prodigal son has returned!
這麼說，浪子回頭了！

Track 352

虛驚一場

a false alarm（名詞）

流行語解密！

a false alarm 本意是假的警報，也就是虛驚一場的意思了。有時用作感嘆詞“false alarm!”（啊，虛驚一場！）

這樣用就對了！

1 John feared that he would not be able to pass the exam, but it was a false alarm.
約翰擔心考試不及格，結果只是虛驚一場。

2 Someone called to say there was a bomb inside the school, but it turned out to be a false alarm.
有人打電話來說，學校裡面有炸彈，結果只是虛驚一場。

Track 353

亂成一團；雜亂無章；亂象叢生

in a (complete) shambles（副詞）

流行語解密！

shambles (名詞) 這個字並非複數，而是單數，最後一個字母 s 是其本身拼字的一部份；它經常以 in a shambles 的介詞片語型態出現，意為「亂成一團；雜亂無章；亂象叢生；凌亂不堪」，當副詞用。必須注意的是，英文還有一個沒有 s 的 shamble，當動詞用，意為「蹣跚；搖搖晃晃地走」。

這樣用就對了！

1 Sarah made a (complete) shamble of the accounts.
莎拉把帳目記得雜亂無章。

2 The meeting ended in complete shambles.
會議結束時亂成一團。

3 Corruption has left the country’s economy in shambles.
貪污腐敗已使這國家的經濟亂象叢生。

像熱鍋上的螞蟻

like a cat on hot bricks（片語）；
like a cat on a hot tin roof（片語）

流行語解密！

like a cat on hot bricks（直譯是：像是貓在熱磚頭上）為英式英語，而 like a cat on a hot tin roof（直譯是：像是貓在熱的錫屋頂上）為美式英語，它們通常位在 be, seem 等連綴動詞之後，都是在表達焦躁不安、坐立難安的意思。

這樣用就對了！

1. Marian was like a cat on hot bricks before her wedding ceremony.
   婚禮前瑪麗安焦躁不安，像熱鍋上的螞蟻。

2. What's the matter with Kelly? She's like a cat on a hot tin roof this morning.
   凱莉怎麼啦？她今天早上坐立難安，像熱鍋上的螞蟻。

輾轉反側

toss and turn （動詞）

流行語解密！

除了 toss and turn，我們亦可用 twist and turn 來表達相同的意思，其中 twist 是「扭轉」的意思，而 toss 則是「丟」的意思。

這樣用就對了！

1. Bernard was tossing and turning all night.
   柏納德整晚輾轉反側，難以成眠。

2. I hoped that I would get a good night's sleep but instead twisted and turned all night long because I was worried about my job.
   我希望一夜好眠，但由於擔心自己的工作，反而整晚輾轉反側，難以成眠。

遍體鱗傷

black and blue （形容詞）

流行語解密！

英文的字面意思為「青一塊，紫一塊」，也就是中文的「遍體鱗傷」了。

這樣用就對了！

1. His son was beaten black and blue at the boarding school.
   他兒子在寄宿學校被打得遍體鱗傷。

2. Her whole body was black and blue after she fell down.
   她摔了下來，跌得渾身青一塊，紫一塊。

★ **boarding school** 寄宿學校

一個巴掌拍不響；一個銅板敲不響

It takes two to tango.

流行語解密！

這句英文字面意思為「要兩個人才能跳探戈」，引伸為「若有爭端或糾紛，雙方都要負責任」，通常用來暗示「吵架時雙方都有錯」，與中文「一個巴掌拍不響」或「一個銅板敲不響」的意思不謀而合。

這樣用就對了！

1. She blames Amy for stealing her husband. Well, it takes two to tango.
   她指責艾美偷了她的丈夫。啊，一個巴掌拍不響。

2. Student: "He hit me first; it wasn't my fault!"
   學生：「他先打我；那不是我的錯。」
   Teacher: "It takes two to tango."
   老師：「一個銅板敲不響。」

★ **blame** [blem] 動 責備

▶ 同義詞：**accuse** [əˋkjuz] 動 控告

▶ 延伸片語：**blame sb. for sth.** 為某事責備某人
take the blame for 為某事承擔責任

★ **fault** [fɔlt] 名 錯誤

揍個半死

knock someone's block off（動詞）

流行語解密！

這是威脅別人時的用語，日常生活中經常會用到，就是威脅要狠揍某人一頓、把某人揍個半死或揍死某人。

這樣用就對了！

1. Paul threatened to knock my block off if I didn't do as I was told.
   保羅威脅我，若不按照他的話去做，就要把我揍個半死。

2. Say that again and I'll knock your block off!
   再說一遍，我就把你揍個半死！

3. I'll knock your block off if I catch you stealing again.
   如果你偷東西再被我抓到的話，我就會揍死你。

★ **knock** [nɑk] 動 敲

★ **block** [blɑk] 名 街區、木塊、石塊／動 阻塞

▶ 延伸片語：**block sth (up)** 阻塞，阻礙

★ **threaten** [ˋθrɛtn̩] 動 威脅

say that again 再說一次，此外 you can say that again 還可能是「（你說的對，所以）再說一次」。

K 得滿頭包

beat/kick/knock the crap/ shit out of someone（動詞）

流行語解密！

K 得滿頭包、狠 K 一頓、狠狠地揍一頓都可用這些英文成語來表示。

這樣用就對了！

1. Shut up or I'll beat the shit out of you!
閉嘴，不然的話我會把你 K 得滿頭包！

2. That guy is such a creep. I really want to knock the shit out of him.
那個傢伙很討厭。我真的很想把他狠狠地 K 一頓。

3. Bill beat the crap out of me after I had dinner with his girlfriend last night.
我昨晚跟比爾的女友共進晚餐後，他把我 K 得滿頭包。

shut up 除了可以用來罵人閉嘴之外，現在也很常在美劇中看到有人驚訝的表情說 shut up，這時意思是「太讓人意外了！」，另外，要人閉嘴還可以用比較有禮貌一點的說法：shut the front door。

★ **creep** [krip] 動 爬行

▶ 相關詞：**creepy** [ˋkripɪ] 形 令人發毛的

「共進晚餐」除了 have dinner 也可以用 eat dinner 喔！

活受罪

a fate worse than death（成語）

流行語解密！

a fate worse than death 是個成語，首次出現在大約 1810 年，但在美國作家愛德加・萊斯・巴勒斯 (Edgar Rice Burroughs) 所創作的《人猿泰山》(Tarzan of the Apes) 一書於 1914 年出版後變得廣為人知。這個成語雖亦可用來表示字面意思，如 Death row is a fate worse than death.（死囚等待行刑生不如死），但現今大多被當作詼諧、幽默用語，用來表示極其難受的事、極不愉快的經歷、活受罪。

這樣用就對了！

1. If you're a teenager, an evening at home with your parents can possibly make you feel like a fate worse than death.
   如果你是個十來歲的青少年，晚上在家和父母待在一起，可能會讓你覺得好像活受罪。

2. Cindy felt that having to move to a small town was a fate worse than death.
   辛蒂覺得，不得不搬到小鎮是個極不愉快的經歷。

★ **teenager** [ˋtinˏedʒɚ] 名 青少年
　▶ 相關詞：**teenage** [ˋtinˏedʒ] 形 十幾歲的

★ **possibly** [ˋpɑsəblɪ] 副 可能地
　▶ 相關詞：**possible** [ˋpɑsəbl̩] 形 可能的

人在屋簷下，不得不低頭

Beggars can't be choosers.

流行語解密！

Beggars can't be choosers 直譯是「乞丐沒有選擇的餘地」，可以解釋成「人在屋簷下，不得不低頭」，另外這句話還有「飢不擇食」的意思，所以翻譯時端賴上下文的意思而定。

這樣用就對了！

1. A: I asked Tom to lend me his computer, and he sent me this old one.
   A: 我要湯姆將他的電腦借給我，而他卻送來這台老舊的電腦。
   B: Beggars can't be choosers.
   B: 人在屋簷下，不得不低頭。

2. Mary: Let me wear your red coat; I don't like the white one you lent me.
   瑪麗：我要穿妳的紅色大衣；我不喜歡妳借我的那件白色的。
   Alice: Beggars can't be choosers.
   愛麗絲：人在屋簷下，不得不低頭。

★ **lend** [lɛnd] 動 借出／名 蓋子

▶ 反義詞：**borrow** [ˋbɑro] 動 借來

▶ 動詞變化：**lend-lent-lent**

▶ 延伸片語：**lend...to sb** 借……給某人

狗急跳牆；忍耐是有限度的
Even a worm will turn.

流行語解密！

這句話源於舊諺"Tread on a worm (or worm's tail) and it will turn."（蠕蟲被踩也會翻騰），也就是中文的狗急跳牆。

這樣用就對了！

1. Even a worm will turn; you had better treat him better.
人急造反，狗急跳牆；你最好對他好一點。

2. You'd better stop shouting at Nina. She's a nice woman, but even a worm will turn.
你最好停止對妮娜大吼大叫。她是個溫文爾雅的女性，但忍耐總有限度。

★ **tread** [trɛd] 動 踩（＋ upon/on）

- ▶ 動詞變化：**tread-trod-trodden**
- ▶ 延伸片語：**tread on someone's heel** 緊跟著（某人）
- ▶ 延伸片語：**tread on someone's corn** 冒犯（某人）
- ▶ 延伸片語：**tread on air** 歡天喜地

挖東牆補西牆；借新債還舊債

rob Peter to pay Paul（動詞）

流行語解密！

To rob Peter to pay Paul 這個成語於大約 1382 年首次出現在英國哲學家約翰 · 威克里夫 (John Wycliffe) 的著作中。舉凡挖（或拆）東牆補西牆、借新債還舊債等類似的意思都可用它來表示。有關這成語的起源有多種說法，其中之一是，英國國教會挪用倫敦聖彼得教堂（St. Peter's Church。注意：梵諦岡聖伯多祿大教堂是 St. Peter's Cathedral）的資產來支付倫敦聖保羅大教堂 (St. Paul's Cathedral) 的修繕費用。

這樣用就對了！

1. Why borrow money to pay your credit card bill? That's just robbing Peter to pay Paul.
   為什麼要借錢來付卡單呢？那只是挖東牆補西牆。

2. Robbing Peter to pay Paul is not a solution. You will still be in debt.
   拆東牆補西牆不是辦法。你仍舊負債。

3. Simon has to take out another loan to pay his debts, robbing Peter to pay Paul.
   賽蒙必須借另一筆貸款來支付欠債，借新債還舊債。

放馬後炮

play Monday morning quarterback（動詞）；play armchair quarterback（動詞）

流行語解密！

Monday morning quarterback 和 armchair quarterback 的意思都是「放馬後炮的人」，兩者可以互換，其中 quarterback 意為「（美式足球的）四分衛」。由於美式足球 (NFL) 的比賽大多在星期天白天進行，星期天晚上只有一場無線聯播網轉播、全美都看得到的比賽。所以，在比賽結束後的星期一早上，你才把自己當成四分衛，說昨天某個四分衛應該怎樣怎樣，那不就是事後諸葛、放馬後炮嗎！至於 armchair quarterback 中的 armchair 並非「扶手椅」（名詞）的意思，它在此係當形容詞用，意為「紙上談兵的；沒有實務經驗的」。armchair quarterback 是仿效 armchair general（紙上談兵的將軍）所創造出來的。至於「馬後炮」及與其同義的事後聰明、事後諸葛或後見之明等說法，還可用 hindsight 或 20/20 vision of hindsight 來表示。不過，hindsight 往往以片語 "with the benefit of hindsight" 的型態出現。20/20 vision（亦可寫成 twenty-twenty vision，讀法亦同）意為「正常的視力；視力完全正常」，比喻為「完全看清楚；看得一清二楚」。

這樣用就對了！

1. I do not agree with playing armchair quarterback on the decision the management made to lay off 100 workers in the last meeting.
我不同意對資方在上次會議中決定裁員 100 人一事放馬後炮。

2. With the benefit of hindsight, we should have acted differently.
我們原本應該採取不同的作法，但這是馬後炮 / 事後諸葛。

Chapter 17

罵人
也是種藝術！

（對某人）比中指

give someone the finger （動詞）

流行語解密！

除 give someone the finger 外，我們亦可用 flip someone off, flip/give someone the bird 來表達完全相同的意思。flip/give someone the bird 原意為「對（演員等）喝倒采，發出噓聲」，但此意思已過時。

這樣用就對了！

1. The citizen gave the soldier the finger.
   有公民對那位軍人比中指。

2. If he mistreats me in this way, I will flipp/gave him the bird.
   如果他像那樣虐待我，我會對他比中指。

Track 366

他媽的

screw it/you/them! （動詞）

流行語解密！

這是罵人的話自不待言，除非怒從心頭起，惡向膽邊生或是怒從心中起，恨從膽邊生，否則別輕易出口以免傷人。動詞 screw 後接名詞或代名詞，就可以表示「他媽的」、「去你（媽）的」等等冒犯的意思。

這樣用就對了！

1. Screw you!
去你媽的！

2. Screw the government!
他媽的，這個政府不是東西！

3. Screw it! If you won't lend me your tablet, I'll just take it.
他媽的！如果你不把你的平板借給我，我就自己拿。

4. A: No, I won't lend you my car.
不，我不會把車子借給你。
B: Well, screw you!
哼，你他媽的不是人！

明褒暗貶

damn somebody/ something with faint praise （動詞）

流行語解密！

damn 在此當動詞用，意為「指責；批評」。

這樣用就對了！

1. Mrs. Wang is very proud of her daughter's achievements, but damns her son's with faint praise.
王太太對她女兒的成就深感驕傲，但對她兒子的成就明褒暗貶。

2. Amy damned Peter with faint praise, calling him one of the best imitators in the world.
艾美對彼得明褒暗貶，稱他是世上最優秀的模仿者之一。

小心眼

petty（形容詞）

流行語解密！

我們亦可用 narrow-minded 來表示相同的意思，指的都是一個人的氣量小、心胸狹窄。

這樣用就對了！

1. Jessica has a petty mind.
   = Jessica is petty.
   潔西卡很小心眼。

2. I can't get along with those narrow-minded women in our company.
   我跟我們公司那些小心眼的女人處不來。

Track 369

小氣鬼

cheapskate（名詞）

流行語解密！

小氣鬼就是小氣、摳門的人。摳門的流行用語是 tightfisted（其他與小氣或摳門同義的字應該也可以用）。

這樣用就對了！

1. Linda is such a cheapskate!
琳達真是個小氣鬼！

2. That cheapskate took his date to a park.
那個小氣鬼竟然把女友帶到公園約會。

Track 370

看到（你）就討厭

can't stand the sight of you

流行語解密！

can't stand the sight of 後接人或事物，即 can't stand the sight of sb/sth（討厭；受不了，見不得），所以「你」可以改成其他人稱，例如：「看到他就討厭」就是 can't stand the sight of him，其中 stand 有時亦可用 bear 來替換。

這樣用就對了！

1. I can't stand the sight of my mom.
現在我看到我媽就討厭。

2. Ever since Tom insulted me, I can't bear the sight of him.
自從湯姆侮辱我以後，我看到他就討厭。

3. Most people can't stand the sight of rats.
大多數人都討厭看到老鼠。

你白活了

You haven't lived.

You haven't lived 經常後接 until ＋子句來表示「你必須做過、吃過、看過或體驗過某事，才算沒有白活」的意思。

這樣用就對了！

1. If you haven't gone bungee jumping, you haven't lived.
如果你沒玩過高空彈跳，那你就白活了。

2. You've never been to a Turkish bath? Oh, you haven't lived!
你從未洗過土耳其浴啊？你真是白活了！

3. You haven't lived until you've played Minecraft.
玩過《當個創世神》你才算沒有白活一場。

★ **bungee jumping** 片 高空彈跳

▶ 相關詞：**extreme sports** 極限運動
▶ 相關詞：**paragliding** 滑翔傘
▶ 相關詞：**gliding** 滑翔（極限運動的一種）
▶ 相關詞：**parkour** 跑酷（在高樓頂端這類城市環境中從事跑步等運動）

Track 372

靠夭；很弱；爛透了

suck（動詞）

流行語解密！

閩南語常常罵「靠么」，除了表示不滿他人的哀號，更常當語助詞表示驚訝、不滿、糟糕。而英文中的 suck 也常用來表示不滿、糟糕。要注意 suck 還有吸吮的意思，但是用來表達糟糕時，只能用現在簡單式。sucks 有時被寫成 SUX。要注意 suck 跟靠夭一樣是不雅的話，使用時要看時間場合喔！

這樣用就對了！

1. "My mom says I should do nothing but study."
「我媽說我只能乖乖唸書。」
"That sucks."
「那很靠夭耶！」。

2. This job sucks. Everyone wants to quit.
這工作很爛。大家都不想幹。

3. This movie sucks. I will give it a negative review on the Internet.
這部電影很爛。我要在網路上給它個負評。

再學多一點！

★ **negative** [`nɛgətɪv] 形 負面的

★ **review** [rɪ`vju] 名 評論

★ **internet** [`ɪntɚ,nɛt] 名 網際網路

▶ 延伸片語：**internet network** 網際電腦網路

龜毛

anal（形容詞）

流行語解密！

「龜毛」就是「吹毛求疵的；愛挑剔的」，亦可用 picky 或 critical 來表示。anal 原意為「肛門的」，但它為何亦可表示挑剔的意思，推測應該跟肛門期人格發展所產生的潔癖等肛門性格 (anal disposition) 有關。

這樣用就對了！

1. Daisy can be anal about keeping her house neat.
   黛西對於保持她家的整潔可是相當龜毛。
2. Harold's the most anal person I've ever met.
   哈洛德是我所見過宇宙最龜毛的人。
3. Sarah's so picky about her clothes.
   莎拉對穿什麼衣服很龜毛／挑剔。
4. Scott's over critical about almost everything.
   史考特對幾乎所有事物都過度龜毛／挑剔。

★ **neat** [nit] 名 整潔的

★ **picky** [ˋpɪkɪ] 形 龜毛的

★ **critical** [ˋkrɪtɪkl̩] 形 評論的

▶ 延伸片語：**be critical of...** 對……挑剔；對……吹毛求疵

★ **disposition** [ˏdɪspəˋzɪʃən] 名 性質

Track 374

流行語解密！

神經病

spaz（名詞）

「神經病」與「瘋子」的意思相近，為負面用語。Spaz 亦可當動詞用，意為「發神經；發瘋」(= freak out)。

這樣用就對了！

1. Kevin is such a spaz.
   凱文真是神經病。

2. People think I'm a spaz.
   大家都認為我是神經病。

3. My computer is spazzing! It crashes very often.
   我的電腦發神經了！它常常當機。

Track 375

流行語解密！

神經質

neurotic（形容詞）

neurotic 亦可當名詞用，意為「有神經質的人；神經過敏者」。

這樣用就對了！

1. Sam and Diana broke up because she is so neurotic.
   山姆和戴安娜分手了，因為她太神經質了。

2. My girlfriend is very neurotic. I've had enough of it!
   我女友非常神經質。我受夠了！

掃興；煞風景

party pooper; wet blanket（名詞）

流行語解密！

a party pooper 和 a wet blanket 都是指「掃興的人；煞風景的人」。不過，它們亦可指使人掃興或煞風景的事物。

這樣用就對了！

1. You are such a party pooper.
   你真是掃興。

2. Robert is not invited to the party because he's such a wet blanket.
   羅伯特沒有被邀請參加派對，因為他總是掃人家的興。

Track 377

壞到骨子裡

rotten to the core（形容詞）

流行語解密！

這片語中的 core 是指蘋果等水果的果心。

這樣用就對了！

1. The whole family are rotten to the core.
   這一家人全都壞到骨子了。

2. Bill said that Kevin is rotten to the core.
比爾說，凱文壞透了。

3. This organization is rotten to the core.
這個組織爛透了。

掛羊頭賣狗肉

sail under false colors （動詞）

流行語解密！

colors 為美式英語的拼法，英式英語為 colours。這個字在此指的是船隻所掛的旗幟。

這樣用就對了！

1. A lot of politicians sail under false colors.
許多政客掛羊頭賣狗肉。

2. That salesman was sailing under false colors. I was sure that she was actually a swindler.
那位業務掛羊頭賣狗肉，我很確定她其實是個騙徒。

★ **politician** [ˌpɑləˋtɪʃən] 名 政治家

★ **salesman** [ˋselzmən] 名 推銷員

★ **swindler** [swɪndlɚ] 名 騙子

跟旗幟相關的還有 with flying colors，意思是勝利，因為以前航海時勝利的船隊會掛上旗幟飄揚，所以衍生為「勝利」的意思囉！

像無頭蒼蠅

like a chicken with its head cut off（成語）

流行語解密！

like a chicken with its head cut off 是美式英語的說法，英式英語是使用 like a headless chicken。這成語經常與 run around 連用來表示「忙得像無頭蒼蠅」的意思。

這樣用就對了！

1. Karen was running around like a chicken with its head cut off trying to do the work of two people.
   卡琳一人要做兩人的工作，忙得像無頭蒼蠅。

2. I've been racing around like a headless chicken all day.
   我整天都忙得像無頭蒼蠅。

學人精

copycat（名詞）

流行語解密！

copycat 指的是什麼東西都要學別人的人，像是小朋友很常會說有人用跟自己一樣的東西是「學人精」。要注意 copycat 有別於 yes man，yes man 是好好先生，別人說什麼都說好。

這樣用就對了！

1. Tom called me a copycat just because I have the same pen as his.
只因我的我有跟他一樣的筆，湯姆就說我是學人精。

2. I like Gary because he's a yes man.
我喜歡蓋瑞，因為他是好好先生。

Track 381

軟柿子

pushover（名詞）

流行語解密！

pushover 這俚語是指容易受影響的人。柿子這種水果的英文是 persimmon，但可別將「軟柿子」（好欺負的人）說成 soft persimmon。

這樣用就對了！

1. I'm kind, but no pushover.
我人好，但並非軟柿子。

2. You should stop being a pushover!
你不應該再做軟柿子了！

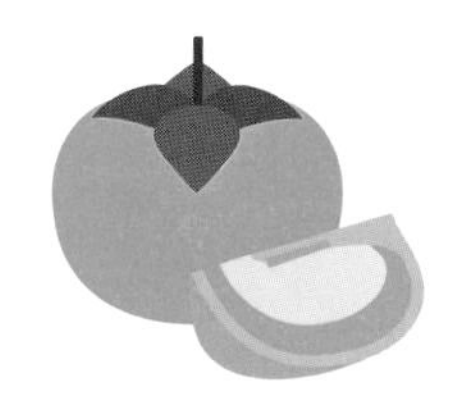

不是……的料
not ... material

流行語解密！

material 本來是「材料」，在此為比喻用法，意為「人才」。

這樣用就對了！

1. Samuel wasn't really police officer material.
山謬真的不是當警官的料。

2. You are not presidential material.
你不是當董事長的料。

Track 383

佔著茅坑不拉屎
a dog in the manger（名詞）

流行語解密！

manger 意為「馬槽」，這成語源自《伊索寓言》(Aesop)，字面意思為「狗佔馬槽」，指狗本身不吃為馬準備的草料，卻又佔著馬槽不讓馬吃。所以，a dog in the manger 是諷刺那些自私的人佔有某些東西，卻不使用，又不肯與人分享。

這樣用就對了！

1. Don't be such a dog in the manger! If you don't want that Barbie doll, give it to Amy.
不要這樣佔著茅坑不拉屎！如果妳不玩那個芭比娃娃，就送給艾美吧。

❷ Cindy borrowed a lot of books from the library but she didn't read any of them. She was really a dog in the manger.
辛蒂從圖書館借了很多書，但一本也沒有看過，真是佔著茅坑不拉屎。

Track 384

金魚腦／貴人多忘事

brain of a goldfish/have a memory/mind/head like a sieve（名詞）,（動詞）

流行語解密！

記得海底總動員的多莉嗎？她總是說 "I suffer from short-term memory loss."（我有短期失意症。）然後說完就忘記了。是的，傳說金魚記憶只有七秒，所以英文也有一句 brain of a goldfish 說人記憶短暫。另外說人健忘還可以用 have a memory/mind/head like a sieve，其中 sieve 意為「篩子」。若記憶力如篩子，則會露洩或漏光，引申為記性極差，非常健忘，即「貴人多忘事」。

這樣用就對了！

❶ My daughter taught me how to use the cellphone twice but I still cannot remember—I've got a memory like a sieve.
我女兒教過我怎麼用手機兩次，但我仍記不住一我真是金魚腦。

❷ I've never known anyone so forgetful—she's got a mind like a sieve.
我還沒見過這麼健忘的人一她真是貴人多忘事。

Chapter 18 閨房情趣！

上床；嘿咻

hanky-panky（名詞）

流行語解密！

hanky-panky 是英文的押韻複合詞 (rhyming compounds)。有些押韻複合詞會隨著時間的演進而產生新的意思，其中 hanky-panky 就是這種舊字新義最典型的實例之一；這個字原義為「欺騙行為；花招」，但現在主要用來指「上床、嘿咻」且被用作性交的委婉語，與中文的用法一樣。

這樣用就對了！

1. Hey you two! Remember: no hanky-panky in my room!
   喂，你們兩個！要記住：別在我房間裡幹那檔事。

2. The hunk and I did the hanky-panky. It was da bomb.
   昨晚我跟那個小鮮肉嘿咻。爽翻了。

Track 386

一夜情

one-night stand（名詞）

流行語解密！

原義為「（僅停留一晚，表演一場的）一夜演出」。

這樣用就對了！

1. I'm not a fan of one-night stands.
   我對一夜情並不熱衷。

2. Some people think one-night stands are immoral.
   一些人認為一夜情是不道德的。

約砲
hook up （動詞）

流行語解密！

指跟伴侶（夫妻或男女朋友）以外的人約定自願發生性行為，旨在尋求相互的滿足，不涉及金錢交易。

這樣用就對了！

1. We've just hooked up a few times.
   我們只約砲了幾次。

2. They hooked up last night after the party.
   他們昨晚在派對後約砲。

3. Hooking up with Martin last night was the biggest mistake in my life.
   昨晚跟馬丁約砲，是我一生中最大的錯誤。

4. Alice and Kent hooked up at a party and Alice ended up getting pregnant.
   愛麗絲和肯特在一場聚會上約砲，結果愛麗絲懷孕了。

炮友

friend with benefits （名詞）

流行語解密！

可以用來表示「炮友」的英文不只 friend with benefits 而已，至少還有兩個片語也可表達完全相同的意思，那就是 friend for cut 和 fuck buddy（複數 fuck buddies），但後者帶有髒字 fuck，似乎沒有 friend with benefits 或 friend for cut 來得文雅。

這樣用就對了！

1. Our relationship has progressed to friends with benefits.
我們已經發展到炮友的關係。

2. Wow, Randy and Amy are more than classmates—they are friends with benefits.
藍迪和艾美不只是同學，他們還是炮友。

★ **progress** [`prɑgrɛs] 動 進展

▶ 相關詞：**progression** [prə`grɛʃən] 名 前進
progressive [prə`grɛsɪv] 形 進步的

★ **benefit** [`bɛnəfɪt] 名 益處、利益

▶ 延伸片語：**benefit by/from** 得益於……

車震

amomaxia （名詞）

流行語解密！

車震亦可用 dogging 來表示，但 dogging 在美國和英國的意思並不相同。在美國，dogging 是指女的躺著而男的在上面或像狗那樣的嘿咻姿勢；在英國，dogging 是指「車震」沒錯，但卻是那種一男一女把車內燈打開、讓車外的人可以一覽無遺地觀看他們炒飯的「車震」，換言之，車內的人有「暴露狂」(exhibitionism)，而車外的人有「窺淫癖」(voyeurism)。因此，dogging 是指有觀眾欣賞、三不五時還鼓掌叫好的「車震」。此外，dogging 在英國也指在車震者不知情的情況下在車外偷窺的行為。

這樣用就對了！

1. Cindy hurt her back after amomaxia with Ken.
   辛蒂與凱恩車震後閃到腰了。

2. Jeff loves to do amomaxia but his girlfriend doesn't.
   傑夫喜歡車震，但是他女朋友不喜歡。

3P

threesome（名詞）

流行語解密！

既然 3P 是 threesome，那麼 4P 不就是 foursome 嗎？沒錯！但別以為因此就可依此類推，5P 是 fivesome，6P 是 sixsome ……等等，因為正規英語並沒有後面這兩個字。

這樣用就對了！

1. The married couple had a threesome with another woman.
   這對夫妻和另一名女子玩 3P。
2. My best friend asked me to join her and her husband for a threesome.
   我的閨蜜要我跟她和她先生一起玩 3P。
3. I want to take part in a foursome.
   我很想玩 4P。

迷姦

drug and rape （動詞）

流行語解密！

drug 在此當動詞用，意為「對……下藥；在……中下藥」，並非服藥（服用一般藥物）的意思。下藥的目的幾乎都是出於不法意圖，如下藥迷昏後劫財或性侵或兩者兼而有之，其中所用的藥物不外乎安眠藥 (hypnotic, sleeping pill/tablet)、麻醉藥 (narcotic，即毒品）或迷魂藥 (knockout drop)—這些名詞在應用上一般大多用複數。

這樣用就對了！

1. The police found a lot of knockout drops in the basement. This made them think that he was using the house to drug and rape female visitors.
   警方在地下室發現許多迷魂藥。這使他們認為他利用這間房子來下藥迷姦女性訪客。

2. The Taiwanese playboy drugged, raped, and filmed celebrities and models.
   這位台灣花花公子下藥迷姦女藝人和模特兒並拍攝性愛影片。

3. Her wine has been drugged.
   她的酒裡被下了藥。

★ **basement** [ˋbesmənt] 名 地下室、地窖

★ **knockout drops** 片 迷魂藥

超夯！英文流行語：這樣說最潮

學校課本學不到的流行語，你的英文 Update 了嗎？！

作　　者　俞亨通
顧　　問　曾文旭
總 編 輯　黃若璇
編輯統籌　陳逸祺
編輯總監　耿文國
行銷企劃　陳蕙芳
執行編輯　賴怡頻
封面設計　吳靜宜
內文排版　張嘉容
文字校對　賴怡頻
音檔校對　賴怡頻
圖片來源　圖庫網站：Shutterstock
法律顧問　北辰著作權事務所　蕭雄淋律師、嚴裕欽律師

初　　版　2018 年 02 月
出　　版　凱信企業集團 - 開企有限公司
電　　話　（02）2752-5618
傳　　真　（02）2752-5619
地　　址　106 台北市大安區忠孝東路四段 250 號 11 樓之 1

定　　價　新台幣 349 元
產品內容　1 書 + 1MP3

總 經 銷　楨彥有限公司
地　　址　231 新北市新店區寶興路 45 巷 6 弄 12 號 1 樓
電　　話　（02）8919-3186
傳　　真　（02）8914-5524

國家圖書館出版品預行編目資料

超夯！英文流行語：這樣説最潮 / 俞亨通著 . -- 初版 .
-- 台北市：開企 , 2018.02
面 ；　公分
ISBN 978-986-94742-8-3（平裝附光碟片）

1. 英語 2. 詞彙

805.12　　106020706

開企，

是一個開頭，它可以是一句美好的引言、
未完待續的逗點、享受美好後滿足的句點，
新鮮的體驗、大膽的冒險、嶄新的方向，
是一趟有你共同參與的奇妙旅程。

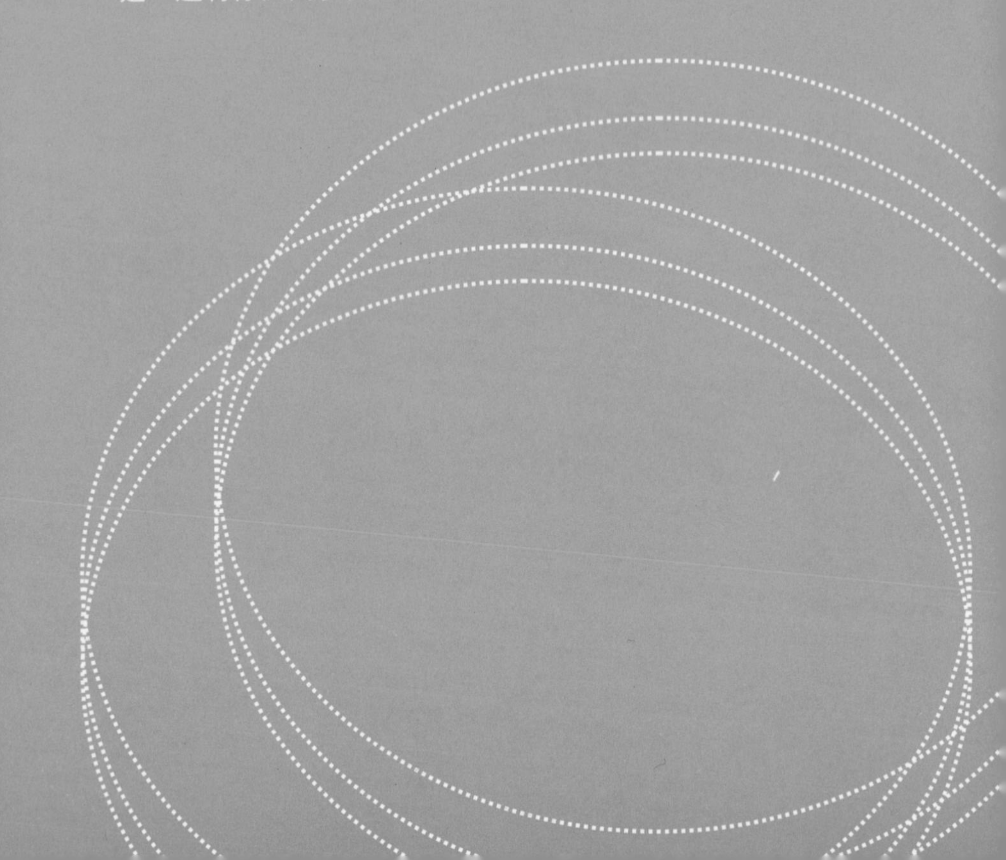